A **CAT'S EYE** Mystery

The HAUNTED MANSION MYSTERY

(Hardcover title: The Treasure Trap)

by
VIRGINIA MASTERMAN-SMITH

SCHOLASTIC BOOK SERVICES
New York Toronto London Auckland Sydney Tokyo

To Ken, Steve, and Mike,
my collaborators and critics

ISBN 0-590-32786-0

Text copyright © 1979 by Virginia Masterman-Smith. Illustrations copyright © 1979 by Scholastic Inc. All rights reserved. Published by Scholastic Book Services, a division of Scholastic Inc.

12 11 10 9 8 7 6 5 4 3 2 1   11   2 3 4 5 6/8

Contents

Angel's Spell	1
Haunted Mansion	17
Partners	35
Spooked	51
We Dig	59
Fiasco	72
We Research	89
Mrs. Jennings's Dessert	110
Jeremiah Cleary's Story	127
We Search	147
Buried Alive	162
Trapped	180
Tapping Again	198
Post Mortem	209

The HAUNTED MANSION MYSTERY

1

ANGEL'S SPELL

Angel Wilson is gone now, and I miss her. I was her best friend. You get to be a girl's best friend when you come close to dying with her, and I came as close to dying with Angel as I ever want to be. I'll tell you about it, but first, I'll tell you about Angel.

Last summer she moved into Old Man Waterman's mansion next door, and I would have gotten a glimpse of her on moving day, except it rained so hard I couldn't go on the attic roof. I've got a swell perch up there where I can see anything, and hear, too. At any rate, once I learned a girl'd moved in next door I figured I hadn't missed much.

Three days later the rain stopped. I was in the kitchen fixing myself a snack for the beach when I happened to look out the window and spy a girl under the old dead tree in the field behind all the houses on my block. She was dancing eerily, spinning in circles, making a bigger circle around the tree.

I'd never seen anything like her outfit — a long, bright-colored skirt with a kerchief to match tied around her head like she was getting rid of lice. I figured it had to be the "new girl." Who else?

I forgot about the beach, grabbed my binoculars, and ran up to the attic roof.

Just as I settled on my perch, the "new girl" stopped, picked up a stick, and waved it at the tree. It was then I noticed Junior Jennings on one of the branches. (Junior lives in the row of houses across the field. He's a terrible tree climber.)

"Junior," the girl sang, "I, the Grand Angel, Knower of All that is to be Known, Seeress of Seeresses, Witch of Witches, do now exhort and warn you to come down from that tree."

To which Junior replied in his most sarcastic tone, "Sure I will. Sure I will."

Angel spun around, stopped, and again pointed the stick at Junior.

"Junior, I, the Grand Angel, Knower of All that is to be Known, Seeress of Seeresses, Witch of Witches, Hexer of Hexers, do warn you. If you don't come down from that tree you will fall."

2

Junior climbed all the higher and called again, "Whooeee, Angel Wilson, Whooeee. Hex me. G'wan and hex me. Make me fall."

Angel began chanting like a prayer.

"I, the Grand Angel, Seeress of Seeresses, Witch of Witches, Knower of All that is to be Known, do declare, Junior Jennings, that you stink at tree climbing. Come down or you will break a leg."

"Sure I will. Sure I will. Whooooeee, Angel Wilson. Whooeeeee. See me break my leg. Whoooeee."

By this time Junior was near the top of the tree. He stopped, grabbed a branch, swung by one arm, scratching himself like a monkey, and halloooed again.

"Whoooeeeee, Angel Wilson. Whoooeee."

At the last "whoooeeeee," the branch broke and Junior tumbled down.

A good thing Angel was there. She ran under him and broke the fall, so all he hurt was his leg. Then she raced across the field to his house and got his mother to call First Aid. After that she grabbed an old quilt from Mrs. Jennings's line and ran back to Junior. She covered him up, sat right in the mud under the tree, and put his head on her lap.

All the time Junior was caterwauling that

Angel had hexed him. When his mother arrived, that's the first thing he told her.

"She hexed me, Mom. Angel Wilson hexed me. She made me break my leg."

Mrs. Jennings was so mad she pulled Angel right from under Junior's head, and his head plopped in the mud.

"I knew you were trouble," she bellowed. "I knew anyone who moved into that house would be trouble. Go home! Go home and don't ever come near my Junior again. What was that name? Angel? Some Angel!"

Mrs. Jennings was so busy yelling at Angel that she forgot to pay attention to Junior who was drowning in the mud. It's a good thing the ambulance arrived, for in another minute Junior would have been a goner.

After that (to pardon the pun), Angel's name was mud in our town. I really think it was more because of that old quilt than Junior's leg.

The quilt that Angel had taken from the Jennings's line was a family heirloom. It had belonged to Mr. Jennings's great-great-great-great grandmother Alice, about a thousand times removed. She'd made it as a young girl while crossing the ocean from England long before the Revolutionary War. Lord Baltimore had slept under it, as well as Lord Calvert and William Penn. Anyway, it's just about priceless, and the Jennings family has papers to prove it. Every year the quilt is the star attraction of the Greater Shore Area Antique Show. Mrs. Jennings had just hung the quilt on the line to air before she brought it to the show.

When Angel covered Junior with it, the quilt got muddy. Since the material was too old to have cleaned, Mrs. Jennings couldn't put it in the show and have everybody say, "Oh, Harriet Jennings, aren't you the greatest," which is a little crazy because the quilt isn't *Mrs.* Jennings's. It's *Mr.* Jennings's.

So Mrs. Jennings was mad.

Mrs. Jennings couldn't be mad at Junior because her Junior could do no wrong, but she had to be mad at somebody, and that somebody was Angel.

So after she got Junior's leg set, Mrs. Jennings called everybody in the Wednesday Afternoon Ladies Bridge Club, and then the PTA. Then she hit Bath and Tennis, and I don't know who else, to say that Angel had deliberately broken Junior's leg, and that if a mother didn't want the same for her kid, she'd better keep him away from Angel.

5

Too bad, 'cause Angel didn't know a soul. I suppose she wouldn't have had a friend if it weren't for me. I'm Billy Beak. I live next door.

Generally I don't have much to do with girls, and even after watching the incident under the tree, I wasn't thrilled about meeting Angel. It was all my mother's fault.

I was in the kitchen pouring orange juice over crushed ice when the telephone rang. It was Mrs. Jennings for my Mom.

Mom was painting in her studio, and might as well have been in Siberia because she never takes a call when she's working, especially from Mrs. Jennings. However, she happened to be working on a picture for Mrs. Jennings, and thought that was what the call was about.

I hung around, hoping it was an invitation to Bath and Tennis. We don't belong because my mom says she'd probably get stuck sitting next to Mrs. Jennings every time she went and that would drive her bananas. Even at the Wednesday Afternoon Ladies Bridge Club my mom feigns sick when she has to play with Mrs. Jennings. I don't know how she gets away with it. Anyone else would be thrown out of the club.

Anyway. Mrs. Jennings always invites Mom to Bath and Tennis because she likes her friends to think that one of her friends is an artist. Mom usually begs off, but sometimes she accepts to make me happy. Not that I like Junior Jennings, but Bath and Tennis is a swell place. It has two Olympic-sized pools and enough tennis courts so that I never have to wait on line to play. It also has shuffleboard and a great coffee shop. Whenever I go, I eat up a storm and put it on the Jennings's tab.

I leaned on the counter while Mom gave all the pat answers to Mrs. Jennings.

"You don't say?"

Pause. Eyes on the ceiling.

"Well, I never."

Pause. Grimace.

"Oh, dear."

Pause. More grimaces.

"Isn't that a shame."

Pause. Choking herself. Tongue hanging out.

"Tsk. Tsk."

It was no use. Obviously we weren't going. I turned to leave when she grabbed my arm so tight I thought I'd wind up in a cast like Junior.

"Wait."

Finally she hung up and released me.

"That screwball," she muttered, glaring at the phone. "Her kid broke his leg and she's blaming the little girl who just moved next door."

My mother calls everybody "little girl" or "little boy," even me. Drives me crazy.

"You mean Junior broke his leg?" I asked.

I couldn't let on I knew, 'cause then she'd know I'd been on the roof. Mom's not too happy about my going on the roof, but it's the best place around to see things.

"Sure did," my mother replied. "Swinging in the dead tree again. Maybe they should put him in a zoo. He seems to think he's a monkey. Too bad he didn't break his head. It might help.

"And that poor child. That poor little girl next door. She won't have a chance in this town with Harriet Jennings gunning for her."

Mom pulled open the refrigerator door and got some cheese. I could tell by the way she slammed the door shut that she was mad.

She chopped a chunk for both of us.

"Have you met her?"

"Who?"

"The girl."

"No. I saw her moving in, but I didn't meet her."

"What's she look like?"

"I don't know. A girl."

"Well, I think you'd better go and meet her. She's going to need a friend."

I couldn't believe that my own mother would suggest such a thing.

"Are you kidding?" I said. "I don't know if I'd like her. Call up Bugsy's mother."

Bugsy Schmitt is a pretty nice girl on our block.

"No. I'm not spreading rumor any further. I want you to go next door and introduce yourself to that girl."

"But, Mom, you don't understand," I said.

"I do understand," my mother snapped. "I understand that you're getting too much like everybody else around here."

I knew what my mother meant. In our town the kids aren't exactly friendly. When a boy moves in, they beat him up a few times, and if he fights back hard enough, he's okay, but a girl — for a month they treat her like she's got cholera. If during that time she does one thing the least bit off, that's it. She may as well pack up and move out, 'cause nobody's going to bother with her. It's mean, I suppose, but that's the way it is.

I'm really not that way. It's just that I can't see sticking out my neck for some girl.

"I'm not going to let that child take abuse because she was unfortunate enough to be around when Junior Jennings fell out of a tree, so you get yourself over there and be nice to her," my mother said.

The tone in Mom's voice told me there was no arguing. I threw my orange ice down the sink and stormed out. She followed while I crossed to the opening in the hedge between our yards. No way to turn back. Not with Mom on the other side of the hedge. I figured that with luck Angel Wilson wouldn't be around. I'd stay awhile, then scoot across the street to Tadpole's. Tadpole was my best friend. He'd swear to any story I later told.

I got through the opening in the hedge and plopped under a tree in Angel's yard. I was pretty burned at my mother for making me play Mr. Nice Guy to some girl.

"Hallo, alo, alo, alo," someone yodeled, but when I turned, nobody was there.

"Aloo," again. Not a yodel this time. More like someone falling off a cliff. It gave me the creeps 'cause I knew too much about the Waterman place.

I could have sworn the voice came from above. I looked up, and sure enough, in the tree was a mop of blond hair swaying. On top of that was a shirt and jeans and two legs bent around a branch.

She spun around the branch like an acrobat until she was sitting on it.

"What's your problem?" she grinned.

"Who says I have a problem?"

"Your face."

"Very funny."

She grabbed the branch with her hands and jumped down.

She was skinny, with long legs, but not as long as mine. Her eyes were big and brown. Her eyebrows black. Her light hair hung past her shoulders.

She wasn't pretty. She wasn't ugly. She was in between. She wore braces on her teeth.

Her jeans weren't like the ones we wear in town. They had stripes on the sides. Her shirt was yellow. It hung out over her jeans. On the pocket was the word "Angel."

When she grinned her eyes lit up.

"I'm Angela Wilson, Angel for short," she said.

Then she raised her arm like a wand and made a circle over me.

"Ah," she said in a deep voice with a peculiar foreign accent. "Angel getting strong vibrations. Very strong. Very strong. Angry."

She closed her eyes, then opened them again.

"Yes. Angel see it now. Angel see you live next door. Something wrong. Something very wrong. What is it?

"Wait! It come clear. Your mother made you come over to meet me. You very mad. Don't be mad. You can go now. Mother has gone back into house."

My first words from Angela Wilson, Angel for short. To tell you the truth I should have known right then that she'd be too much for me, gotten up, and walked away. I'm not quick sometimes. I stayed.

"Brilliant deduction, Lady Clairvoyant," I said, "especially since you saw the whole thing from the tree. Now, since you're so smart, what's my name?"

She dropped her arm and stared down at me.

"Let's see," she said, her tone returning to normal. "You've red hair, and freckles. Turn your cap around so I can see the front."

I turned the peak of my Little League cap to the front, so she could see the letter on it.

"Mmmm . . . 'S.' Must be for Sean with *your* red hair. That's it. You're a Sean. I guess your last name's Irish, too. Like Maloney or Mahoney or something."

"No," I snickered. "I'm about as Irish as the Fourth of July."

(Actually I'm Heinz, fifty-seven varieties. A little Scotch, a little Italian, a little Lithuanian, a little Greek, a little English, and then some — my mother calls me full-blooded American.)

I took off my cap.

"This," I told her, "is a Little League cap. The 'S' stands for Shadow Lawn, the name of the town in which you now live. Don't you know a Little League cap when you see one? Where have you been all these years?"

"Not here," Angel sighed, her face clouding. "I haven't been here in a long time. Last year it was England. The winter before that, Mexico, then Haiti, and France, and Japan, and I don't know where else. It gets too hard to keep track."

"What were you doing in all those places?" I asked.

"I'm with my father. He's a treasure hunter."

"A treasure hunter? What does he hunt?"

"Treasures, of course," Angel smirked. "What do you think? You know, gold and all that good stuff."

"Gosh," I said. "It must be great to hunt treasures."

"I wouldn't know," she scowled. "I never go. I just get plopped with Miss Sally and *he* goes."

She looked so dejected I had to say something nice.

"That's a good trick you did."

"What trick?"

"Just now, in the tree. Spinning around the branch."

"Oh, that," Angel shrugged. "Mmmm. It's fun, but you have to know what tree you're on. That kid Junior is a jerk. He shouldn't have played monkey in a dead tree."

I laughed. Junior Jennings was a jerk, but nobody dared say it, 'cause his mother ran the town.

"You'd better not let Junior hear you call him a jerk," I said. "He'll run home to Mama."

"He already did, I suppose," Angel grinned.

14

She fell to the ground, holding her leg as if it were broken.

"Mommy, she hexed me," she mimicked Junior's high-pitched caterwaul perfectly.

Then she sat up.

"Hmph. Too bad about him. Any kid mean enough to blame me for his stupidity isn't worth my time."

"Just the same, you've got problems," I told her.

She tied the lace on her sneaker.

"Then you'd better not stick around, or you'll have problems, too," she said.

"I stick where I please," I snapped.

"Do you really mean that?" she asked. "I mean . . . really?"

"Of course I mean that," I said. "Really."

She broke into a grin and bowed like a Chinese waiter.

"Then I'm pleased to make you my first friend in Shadow Lawn, New Jersey, U.S.A. Now that's something."

She thought for a minute.

"You know, you never did tell me your name."

I smiled.

"Billy Beak."

"Billy Beak. How do you do, Billy Beak?" she said, reaching for my hand.

"Come!"

The next thing you know she'd pulled me up, and we were bounding toward her house, the great big house that had been empty since Old Man Waterman disappeared seven years ago. The house was haunted, and I knew it. As Angel opened the door I shivered.

2

HAUNTED MANSION

Before I tell you why I knew that Angel's house was haunted I have to tell you about the man who lived there before her, Old Man Waterman.

Seven years ago, September, Old Man Waterman disappeared. Before that day he had lived in the house next to me for as long as I could remember. He never went anywhere. He never talked to anybody. And he *hated* kids.

Once, when I was little, I had the misfortune to throw my ball into his yard. I ran to get it, and Old Man Waterman burst out his front door, like he'd been waiting for me all the time. He was swinging a stick, screaming like a banshee for me to get off his land.

"Little snoop," he shouted. "Sneaky little brat."

I ran for my life. I would have kept running right around the earth, if my mother hadn't come out to see what the commotion was about. I crashed right into her, crying to beat the band. She picked me up and stormed right back to Waterman's.

He was still outside, mad as ever, swinging his stick and jumping up and down.

"Listen, you old goat," my mother said, "don't you ever speak to my Billy like that again."

"Don't call me an old goat," Waterman shouted.

"Then leave my son alone," Mom shouted back.

"Then keep your son off my property," Waterman shouted.

"He went for the ball you stole," my mother shouted back. "Give him back his ball."

"I'll give him nothing. What's on my property is mine."

"Then you'll pay. You'll pay. You'll see," Mom shouted.

Of course Old Man Waterman never paid for the ball. My father bought me another one that night. He told me never to go near the Waterman place, that the man was plumb crazy.

And I never did. From that day on I kept myself as far from Old Man Waterman as I could. I wouldn't even go on his sidewalk, never mind his grass.

I wasn't the only kid Old Man Waterman went after. He called the police on Junior Jennings 'cause he crossed through his yard on his way home from Tadpole's. Mrs. Jennings had a conniption, but the police said that the man had a right to his own land, which threw Mrs. Jennings into a worse fit, for reasons you'll learn later.

You might think the kids in town would have given Old Man Waterman a hard time, since he was so mean, but they didn't. After Junior's fiasco, everybody kept off that property. They were too scared of him. I think it was his eyes.

They were ordinary gray, but they never changed expression — an angry stare, angry, angry all the time — anger with a threat behind it.

I've seen that anger in other people's eyes. I suppose I even have it in my eyes at times. But Old Man Waterman's never ended: glass-burning anger, like a smoldering fire that refused to go out.

Everybody felt it. When Old Man Waterman walked down the street people actually crossed to the other side to avoid his glare.

He didn't go out often, just now and then for groceries, pushing a wheelbarrow before him. He walked stooped, as if he'd spent his life bent over. An army coat, buttoned even in summer, hung to his ankles. The top of his head was bald, but on the sides his hair hung in strings, chopped at the shoulders.

I've said before that Old Man Waterman hated kids, but he didn't like adults any better. My mother tells the story of the Christmas she brought Old Man Waterman a fruitcake.

His porch was dark as night. My mother had to knock five times before he answered, and when he did, he slammed the door in her face before she could say "Merry Christmas."

That was Old Man Waterman. He never celebrated a Christmas or a Fourth of July, or Halloween, or anything.

But he had money. He had lots of money, and that's a fact. Tadpole's father is the president of the bank, and he can vouch that eight years ago, Old Man Waterman came into his bank and cashed one million dollars in bearer bonds.

Darn near the whole town was there (at a distance) to watch him roll that money home in his wheelbarrow. The bank sent two guards to make sure he didn't get robbed on the way. As if anyone could rob him with the whole town watching.

When they got to his house the guards wanted to carry the money in, but Old Man Waterman wouldn't let them touch it. He himself carried every sack up the front steps and into the hall. Then he let the guards bring the wheelbarrow to the door, but he himself took it into the house.

He locked and bolted the door behind him, and that's the last anyone saw of Old Man Waterman.

The next day Mike Callahan's father got a call to board up the place. Took him three days, and when he'd finished he found his pay in the mailbox.

After some weeks, the neighbors were worried. Not that they liked Old Man Waterman, but they were afraid he'd been robbed and murdered.

Tadpole's father said it was nobody's business, but they called the police anyway.

The police finally broke through the front

door. They went from cellar to attic, every room, every closet, but they found no sign of Old Man Waterman or his money. So they reboarded the place and waited.

A few nights later, my father saw lights through the cracks in Waterman's boarded windows. So did a lot of other people. Again they called the police, but this time they refused to come. They said it was none of their business.

Strange. They wouldn't come that night, but the next day they drove by and checked the property.

As a matter of fact, the police often checked the Waterman property, and heaven help the person on it. Bugsy Schmitt, who was never afraid of Old Man Waterman, got caught trying to steal boards from a window for her doghouse. She almost went to jail.

It wasn't just lights people saw at Waterman's. They heard noises, too. Once they heard an awful crash, like a big piece of furniture falling down, but the police refused to go into the house and check it out.

That was it. Word spread that the Waterman place was haunted. The Supernatural Society came down to check the rumor, but the police wouldn't let them inside. They sent them to Tadpole's father, and he sent them away.

What Tadpole's father had to do with the Waterman place I didn't know.

Last winter the county put the Waterman property up for sale, to pay back taxes. My father wanted to buy for an investment. He'd never believed those ghost stories.

My mother wouldn't let him. She said there was trouble with that house. My father said my mother was crazy and they had a big argument.

My mother won. We didn't buy the house.

Just as well, for the house *was* haunted. Tadpole and I were in it last Halloween. (What happened to us that night we'd sworn to secrecy.)

It was getting late. We tricked or treated for a while, but the little kids on the street were getting on our nerves.

We didn't want to go home, so we decided to break into Waterman's house. Halloween was a perfect time for it, and since we didn't believe those ghost stories any more than our fathers did, we thought it would be fun.

Luckily, I had one of those Halloween

flashlights with a skull head. The night was dark — a sliver of a moon and no stars. It would be like ink in Waterman's.

We snuck around the back and pried open a cellar window. It wasn't hard — the wood was rotting with age.

As soon as the first board was off we could smell the cellar. Dead mildew, if there is such a thing. We held our noses and jumped down. Spiders crawled all over us. We shook them off and pushed through the webs to the stairs. They creaked like something in a horror movie, but we made it to the first floor, and found ourselves in a great hall. It was big as my living room, dining room, and kitchen put together, and the ceiling was so high my light couldn't reach it.

In the middle of the hall stood an enormous staircase. I was for going up, but Tadpole held me back. I pulled away from him.

Just as my foot hit the first step, I heard a voice.

"Billyyyyybeeek. Youuuuu. Billyyyyyy-beeek."

I remembered that voice. How could I forget? Old Man Waterman's — just as on the day he'd hollered at me. But this time he wasn't screaming. He spoke slowly and low. The same voice. No matter how he toned it, it was the same voice.

"Billyyyybeeeeeek. Billyyyybeeeeek."

I reached back for Tadpole.

"Did you hear that?"

"What?"

"The voice!"

"What voice? You're crazy. I didn't hear a thing."

I figured my imagination was playing tricks with me. I let Tadpole go.

Then I heard something bounce on the steps. When Tadpole grabbed me, I knew he'd heard it, too.

It bounced faster and faster. Down the steps faster and faster. Louder and louder. Closer and closer.

We were too scared to move. We held one another and waited — for what, we didn't know. Like pillars we waited while the bounces vibrated in our ears.

Then, as quickly as they'd started, the bounces stopped. Something rolled to my feet. I let go of Tadpole long enough to shine my light on it.

It was a ball! A pink rubber ball like the

one I'd lost a long time ago on Waterman's lawn.

Then I heard the voice again.

"Here's your ball, Billyyyyyy."

I looked at Tadpole.

"Did you hear it that time?" I whispered.

"Yes."

I peered up the stairs, shining my light as far as it would go.

They were empty.

"Commm, Billyyyy. Don't be afraid. Commmm."

Was it truly Old Man Waterman talking to me? What did he want? Hadn't he always hated me? Hadn't he called me a "sneaky brat" when I was little? Why was he talking so softly now?

Over and over the voice repeated itself.

"Commmmm, Billyyyyy. Billyyyyy, commmm. Commmm."

I held the light so tightly it's a wonder the plastic didn't crack. After a time I had to steady one hand with the other, both were shaking so.

Now the voice rang in my brain.

"Commm, Billyyyyy. Commmm."

I attempted to raise one foot, to start up the stairs after the voice but I couldn't move.

I had to stop the voice. Maybe if I answered. . . .

My lips cracked as I opened them.

"What do you want?"

I waited for a reply.

"What do you want?" I repeated.

Still no answer.

"It's gone away," Tadpole sighed in relief.

I said nothing. Instead, I turned my light to the ball at my feet, the pink rubber ball I'd played with when I was little.

"Why do you suppose he gave it back?" I asked.

I bent to get it, but Tadpole grabbed my arm.

"Don't touch! You'll make contact!"

I stiffened.

Tadpole was right. That's what Old Man Waterman wanted. He wanted me to touch the ball. He wanted me to touch the ball and make contact with him!

For a fleeting second I saw his eyes before me. Those angry eyes. The burning anger that had frightened me so many times.

There was only one thing to do. Get out!

We bolted for the cellar, then to the window. I don't know how we fit through it together.

I don't remember. The next I remember we were both back in my yard.

Even the dark night was brighter than that house. The sliver moon silhouetted the trees. Our kitchen light glowed, lighting the back porch and shadowing the bushes in front of us.

We threw ourselves on the grass. Crickets chirped. Bugs bit us. The purr of a car came from the street in front of the house.

Finally I could talk.

"It *is* haunted," I said. "It isn't a rumor, it's a fact."

"My father'd never believe us," Tadpole replied.

"Nor mine," I said. "Maybe my mother."

"My father'd have a fit if he knew we went in there," Tadpole said. "Maybe he'd turn *me* into a ghost."

Spitting on our fingers and joining them, we made a pact of secrecy. To be more certain, Tadpole cut his wrist, then mine. We joined the blood.

"I'll never breathe a word, hope to die," Tadpole said.

"Nor I, hope to die," I added.

If I'd known then what was to happen, I'd have never uttered those words.

Strange thing is that although I'd stayed clear of the Waterman house, until Angel, I'd almost managed to forget Halloween. I suppose you could say I'd packed it in the part of my memory that doesn't want to work.

Then Angel brought me back into that great hall.

It was bright that day. The boards were no longer on the windows, and light beamed in. A crystal chandelier gleamed over us.

In daylight I could see up the staircase.

No wonder Tadpole and I never found the ceiling. The room was vaulted. There were two landings under wide crossbeams, and above them I could see more stairs winding further up.

I shuddered. Surely, I'd have been killed had I gone up to Old Man Waterman.

"Is something wrong?" Angel asked.

Her words startled me. I'd been so wrapped in thought, I'd forgotten she was there.

"Wrong? What do you mean?"

"Is something wrong? You look like you've seen a ghost."

Whatever made her say that? Maybe she *was* a witch.

"You're white as one," she continued.

I felt my face. It was damp with perspiration.

"Maybe I did," I replied. "This place sure spooks me."

"Not you, too?" Angel groaned, plunking on the bottom step. "Oh, dear. I thought you were different."

"What do you mean 'different'?"

"I mean that everywhere we go in this town somebody says, 'So you're the ones who bought the haunted house.' Then they look at us like *we're* ghosts. Makes me sick."

"The house *is* haunted," I said. "You'd better watch out."

I felt the least I could do was warn her, since I was her only friend.

"Baloney," she said, tossing her blond hair behind her. "I've been here almost a week and haven't seen hide nor hair of a ghost. If we have one, it's mighty shy."

"Maybe the ghost isn't interested in you," I said.

"Why not?"

" 'Cause you never knew him."

"And you did."

"Of course," I said, importantly.

"And he's interested in you."

30

"Of course."

Angel took a deep breath and let the air out slowly.

"Not that I want to hurt your feelings, Billy," she said, "but the fact is that if a house is haunted, the ghost isn't particular about whom it bothers."

"And you're an expert on ghosts, I suppose," I snorted.

"I know a little. We had one in the house we rented in England. It drove us bats. We finally had to move out."

She waited for me to question her about her English ghost, but I didn't. Mine was more important.

I told her about Halloween.

As I talked, Angel's eyes grew wider. I could tell she was impressed, so I made the story as good as I could.

When I came to the part about the ball bouncing down the steps I got so involved that I nearly scared myself all over again.

Suddenly Angel threw back her head and burst into laughter.

On and on she laughed — giggles, and spurts, and chokes, and sighs, and "ha, ha, ha, ha's," that ended in sighs and more giggles.

"I don't think it's funny," I said, when she'd stopped for breath. She looked at me and started all over again.

I couldn't believe it. Here I was trying to save her life, and she was laughing. So much for Angel Wilson. Disgusted, I headed for the door.

"Wait, Billy," she called as I turned the knob. "Don't be mad. Give me a chance to explain."

"So explain," I said, without turning around.

"Oh, come over here and sit. Come on now. Please."

I turned, but didn't take a step back.

She grinned at me, making her eyes crinkle, but she didn't wait for me to come before she started.

"Ho," she sighed. "That was terrible, just terrible. I know I shouldn't have laughed. It's just that you were so sure Old Man Waterman threw the ball down to you. You looked so scared telling about it, that I *had* to laugh.

"Billy, Old Man Waterman didn't throw the ball at you. The ball was there all the time. Frankly, it's a wonder that only one ball came down the stairs that night. When my father first came in here, thousands of balls bounced down these stairs. They kept coming and coming at him so fast that he said he thought he was a bowling pin. There were all kinds of balls — big, little, tennis, golf, you name it. When they stopped, the whole floor was covered with them."

"You're kidding," I said.

"Would I kid about something like that?" she replied, all smiles gone. "We couldn't understand where all those balls came from, but when we heard what a dizzy Old Man Waterman was, we figured he'd set them there to scare intruders away."

"But when could he have set them?" I asked. "They weren't in the house when the police checked the place."

"Then he set them after the police left."

"He wasn't around after they'd left. He'd disappeared. Remember?"

"But people saw lights and heard noises. Maybe that was he. Maybe he was hiding all the time."

"Where?" I asked. "There wasn't a spot the police didn't look."

"I don't know. It's got to be around here somewhere."

"And maybe he's still hiding there now," I said. "Did you consider that? Did you consider that Old Man Waterman might be here in this house, and that some night he might come out and murder you?"

I figured that would get her. Really shake her up, and she deserved it. She had no right to laugh at my story.

But Angel wasn't scared. She stood up, smiled at me, smiled at the four walls and the ceiling, and said loud and clear, *"As long as you don't bother us, Mr. Waterman, you're welcome."*

3

PARTNERS

I wouldn't venture into Angel's house again until I had a long talk with Miss Sally. She was Angel's housekeeper, a nice lady — a little plump — with light brown fluffy hair. When Angel was born she'd come to be her nurse, and never left her because Angel's mother died soon after.

Confidentially, I didn't believe that Angel had been to all those countries. And more confidentially, I didn't believe in Angel's story about the English ghost. Even more confidentially, I didn't believe that the house was full of balls when Mr. Wilson first entered it, and that they'd all come tumbling down on him. In short, I didn't believe much of what Angel said.

We sat on the back lawn at a card table covered with linen and small china plates. Miss Sally brought out a covered dish of hot crumpets freshly toasted and buttered. I'd never before had them, and can't explain the taste, except that it was sort of a cross between sweet pancakes and crullers.

"Some people put jam on them," Miss Sally smiled, placing a knife before me.

Angel grinned and took a bite. Miss Sally went in and came out with a teapot wrapped in its own knitted sock.

I guess I looked surprised that she'd put a sock on a teapot, but Angel explained.

"It's a tea cozy. Keeps the tea warm."

"Nothing worse than cold tea," Miss Sally added.

I'd never been served tea and crumpets on a linen tablecloth in a backyard before. Frankly I didn't know what to do. When Angel and Miss Sally put milk and sugar in their tea, I followed, even though my mother uses lemon in hers.

"Delicious," said Miss Sally, obviously enjoying her own fare. "Have another, Billy."

Much obliged. I took four. Miss Sally sure could cook. I figured if my mother spent a quarter more time in her kitchen, and a quarter less in her studio, she might come up to half of this.

"Now," Miss Sally said, wiping her lips daintily after a munch, "what seems to be your problem?"

I was terribly uncomfortable with Angel sitting right there. I wasn't used to telling a person directly that I believed she was a liar.

"Billy doesn't believe a word I've said. He thinks I've made everything up — the balls in the hall, and the English ghost, and I don't know what else. I'll bet he thinks I really made Junior Jennings break his leg."

"No. I don't think that," I defended. "I saw the whole thing. But the rest, how do you know I don't believe you?"

"I can see it in your eyes."

"You can read a lot in a person's eyes," Miss Sally agreed. "Well, now. Where do you want to begin?"

"Begin at the beginning and end at the end. Wake up, Dormouse. Wake up," Angel giggled.

Lord. I was at a mad tea party. Wasn't I? If the kids in the neighborhood ever saw this. . . .

I gulped another crumpet and asked, "What about the English ghost?"

"Not a ghost, a poltergeist," Miss Sally

sighed. "That was dreadful. We did everything we could to please it, but it wouldn't be nice. We talked to it. We sang to it. We set a place at the table for it. I even put fresh towels in the bathroom for it, but it wouldn't be nice. Kept messing the house and breaking glasses. But the worst was the garbage, right in the middle of the kitchen floor. Filthy, dirty poltergeist. Spoiled. That's what it was. Spoiled.

"I don't know how many maids quit in the three months we were there. I couldn't count them all. And poor Angel. She couldn't get a bit of sleep at night. The poltergeist kept pushing her out of bed. At first we thought perhaps Angel was in the poltergeist's bed, so she changed rooms, but then it wanted every bed Angel slept in. Poor child."

"Then Daddy came home from Northumberland and sent me to that school, instead of bringing me back with him like he'd promised. As if it were my fault the poltergeist did all those things," Angel glowered.

"That wasn't it at all, child," Miss Sally corrected. "Your father was worried about all the school you'd missed because you were too exhausted in the morning to go. And he wanted you to have peace for the rest of the year."

"Some peace," Angel snapped, "with the poltergeist right after me."

"You mean the school was haunted, too?" I asked.

"You bet. Bad enough to be in boarding school, but I had to put up with that!"

"I know," Miss Sally cajoled, "but you shouldn't have sprayed shaving cream in the head mistress's slippers."

"You did that?" I asked.

"I did, and more," Angel replied defiantly.

"She did," Miss Sally groaned. "She put salt in the sugar barrel and pepper in the tea. The whole school came down with a bad case of bellyache and Angel was dismissed."

I couldn't keep from laughing. When I noticed Angel shaking with giggles I figured I could let out a roar. Even Miss Sally chuckled.

"I believe your father got the idea," she said, "and not a day too soon. I was dying of loneliness for you."

She gave Angel a more loving look than I've ever seen, even from my own mother, and Angel basked in it.

"And what about all those countries?" I

asked, after the laughter subsided. "Has she really been to France, and Japan, and Mexico, and all that?"

"Angel has been on every continent of the world save Antarctica," Miss Sally boasted. "Before she was five she could speak five languages. Unfortunately she never got them straight. She used words from all five in every sentence. What a time we had understanding her."

"Should have taught me sign language," Angel remarked.

"Yes. Well, we won't have that problem anymore. We're back in the states now, and we're going to stay."

"I'm not. I'm going on Daddy's next treasure hunt."

"Oh, dear. I thought we got that all ironed out. I thought you said you'd like to live in a little town in America."

"Well, I don't anymore," Angel said, with vehemence. "And I don't want to live anywhere else, either. I want to go with Daddy."

It looked to me as if we'd have a fight on our hands. Angel's face was very tight. I decided to change the subject.

"What about the balls on the stairs when

Mr. Wilson came in?" I asked. "Did they really attack him the way Angel says?"

"Did they attack him? His legs were black and blue for days. And it took six garbage cans to be rid of the balls.

"Come to think of it," she added to Angel, "we shouldn't have thrown them away. We should have donated them somewhere."

"I guess so," Angel agreed.

I hope to die, but that is what transacted the day I had tea with Angel and Miss Sally. I felt terrible for not believing Angel in the first place. Still, the guilt didn't keep me from getting the creeps anytime I entered her house. After all, I'd *heard* the Waterman ghost, and nothing Angel said could dissuade me from the knowledge that it was there.

"It must have been your imagination. Imagination can play terrible tricks," she said anytime I mentioned it.

Let Angel think what she liked, her house gave me the creeps. I would never have gone in, except that I felt sorry for her. Mrs. Jennings had bad-mouthed her well, and she didn't have a friend.

I kept telling her that after a while the kids would forget about Junior's leg, that things would be better. She'd laugh and say it didn't matter, but I knew it did, for when she laughed it was only her voice.

Miss Sally was right. You can read a lot in a person's eyes.

Angel never came to the beach with me. She must have known that bringing her would put me in a sticky situation with the kids. I told her that she didn't exactly have to go *with* me, that she could come down alone and I would introduce her, but she said she wasn't much interested in beaches anymore, which didn't make sense because she'd swum at just about every beach there was.

She said Australia was best. The water was warm and calm. Of course, she always went where they had shark nets.

One day when I returned from the beach, she was waiting for me. She was so excited.

"Come see what I found. You won't believe it," she said.

I followed her into her house and up the stairs. Her room was on the third floor at the end of a hall with so many doors off either side, I could never get the count.

It was a big room, and pretty, I guess, if you were a girl. She had brand new wallpaper, pink and blue, and her carpet was white. She used the room as her office.

I once asked her if Miss Sally didn't holler at her when she got the carpet dirty, but she said she wasn't in her room long enough to get anything dirty, and that was the truth.

She never slept there. She took turns in all the other bedrooms, a different room each night, and Miss Sally liked that, 'cause she didn't have to see that the sheets were changed more than once a season.

Of course, the day maid had trouble finding which bed to make in the morning, but Angel solved that. She stuck a big gold star on her door, so all the maid had to do was find the star and she had her bed.

Angel had a huge desk, and went right to it, pulling out a tin box. She took a key from a string around her neck and opened it. She pulled out a piece of yellow paper.

"Look," she beamed, "I found this in the library. My father doesn't know I have it."

When I looked at the paper, I didn't see why he'd care if she did. It was a sketch of a big tree with a moon behind it, and a long shadow in front of it with some lines in front of that. It looked like something a primary-school kid would make when the teacher wasn't looking.

"What's so great about this?" I asked.

"It's a treasure map!" Angel exclaimed.

"Don't be silly. Where's the skull and cross-bones? Every treasure map has to have a skull and crossbones."

"That's just in stories," Angel said disgustedly. "I've seen lots of treasure maps without. My father showed them to me. He's working on one now in Egypt. It's a pharaoh's treasure. It's all in hieroglyphics. He's trying to figure them out."

"You mean your father's in Egypt?" I asked.

I'd wondered where her father was. He never seemed to be around.

"No. He's at the Museum of Natural History most of the time. And when he's not there he's in our library downstairs. But he's going to Egypt soon. I hope he takes me."

"What are you worrying about?" I asked. "Hasn't he taken you everywhere else?"

"Sure," Angel replied. "He takes us, dumps us off, and goes on his hunt. I'm so sick of sitting around while he's having all the fun."

"What about England? You didn't exactly sit around with that poltergeist."

44

"We couldn't sit. The chairs kept flying all over the place."

"What are you going to do about the ghost in this house?" I asked.

"Not that again," Angel sighed. "How many times do I have to tell you, Billy, that there isn't any ghost. I've been up night after night waiting for one to come, but there isn't any. This house isn't haunted, but there is a treasure, and I have found the map to it. Now all I have to do is figure it out and I can find the treasure. Once I've proven I'm a treasure hunter too, my father will take me with him on his hunts. I just have to prove myself. That's all."

Angel didn't spend more time mooning about hunts with her father.

"Look!" she said, pointing to the full moon on the map. "You see that shadow in front of the tree? It's directed at my house. That's these lines."

She pointed to vertical lines in the foreground.

"I think the treasure is somewhere on a path between the tree and the house. There is a path already between the dead tree in the field and my house. Maybe it's that one."

She was talking about a footpath between her house and the field. When Angel's house was part of an estate, there was a guest house in the field, and the path led to it.

I didn't agree. The tree on Angel's map was full and leafy, but the tree in the field was dead.

"I knew it was too easy," Angel groaned. "A treasure hunt is never that easy. I suppose we'll have to wait for the next full moon to figure this out."

"We might not do it even then," I said. "The moon doesn't stay in the same place all year. It all depends on which month this map was drawn."

Angel studied the map thoughtfully.

"We've got to start somewhere," she said in exasperation. "The map wasn't drawn in winter. It could have been the summer."

"Or spring or fall," I noted.

"We'll chance it was summer. Treasure hunters take a lot of chances."

She folded the map and returned it to the box.

"Want to be my partner?" she asked.

"For what?"

"For the treasure hunt."

All this talk about a treasure was a lot of fun, but I had no idea Angel *really* meant it. Sure there was a million dollars missing, but that map wasn't the clue to it.

"This has to be the clue," Angel said. "Why else would it have been in the library?"

"Maybe a kid drew it."

"Did you ever hear of a kid in Waterman's library?"

She had a point.

"You think Old Man Waterman hid his money and then disappeared?" I asked. "Why wouldn't he have taken his money with him?"

"He was probably so rich he didn't need it. Anyway, he was sick of getting mad at everybody in this town, so he went somewhere else to be mad."

"I don't know," I said. "He was mad here for an awful long time."

"It doesn't matter. What matters is that we have a map for the treasure. Wouldn't it be great if we could find it? But I'll need help digging."

I knew it. She wanted me to help her dig holes. Well, she had another guess coming. I wasn't going to dig for make-believe treasure on a make-believe map because she wanted to be a treasure hunter.

"Count me out," I said.

"But think how rich we'll be when we find it," Angel argued. "One million dollars! A thousand thousand dollars! That's four million quarters! That's ten million dimes! That's twenty million nickels! Not to mention pennies. I haven't figured the pennies."

"At one hundred pennies to the dollar it is exactly one hundred million pennies, which will fill this room and then some," I said.

"See? I knew I picked the right partner. You're almost as smart as I am," Angel exclaimed.

What did she mean "almost as smart"? I was the one who'd figured out the pennies, not she.

I said as much, but Angel didn't hear. She'd pulled a paper from her desk and shoved it in the typewriter. Humming to herself, she began picking at the keys with one finger.

I flopped on the bed and stared at the ceiling. How was I going to get out of this?

Pretty soon she pulled the paper out, smiled at it, and brought it to me.

"How's this?" she asked, flopping at my side. "Pretty professional, huh?"

It *was* impressive.

Treasure Hunters, Inc.
Angela Wilson, President
Billy Beak, Vice President

"Wait a minute," I said. "Why can't we both be presidents? We're partners, aren't we?"

"Can't have two presidents," Angel grimaced. "Bad business. Besides, it's my property, it's my treasure map, and it's my idea. Actually I'm giving you a good deal. Half a million is nothing to sneeze at."

She had a point.

The contract went on to say that we were full partners and would share fifty-fifty any treasure found, including the Waterman money. At the bottom was a space for both our signatures.

Angel gave me her word that we wouldn't roam her house at night. Maybe the Waterman ghost didn't bother *her*, but I wasn't sure what it would do if it caught up with *me* again.

I signed, then Angel did. We shook hands. She locked the contract in her tin box with the map.

"What now?" I asked.

"Wait for the full moon," she replied. "And by the way, don't tell anybody about the map. It's our secret."

4

SPOOKED

After signing the partnership, I didn't see Angel for a week. Actually, I forgot about her, because I was busy working out with Tadpole.

You see, Mike Callahan had pitcher's elbow. Since I was catcher, and Tadpole's best friend, it was only right I help him get Mike's place on the team.

The tryouts were for Sunday night. Everyday we worked for as long as Tadpole's arm could stand it, so that by the time Sunday rolled around, he was terrific. I signaled, and he zipped whatever I called right in. I don't know which of us was prouder when he got picked as pitcher.

That night I went to bed feeling superb. Over and over I dreamed of our first game, when Tadpole would show his stuff. I pictured the batters going down in order. One. Two.

Three. Zip. Zap. Zip. Six straight innings. And in the end, when Tadpole had pitched his shut-out, I could see the kids swamping him, whopping him on the back, telling him he was the greatest. And I'd stand there and smile while Tadpole said, "It's all Billy's fault. He's the one who trained me. You ought to thank Billy."

And the kids would whop my back and put me on their shoulders, and put Tadpole on their shoulders, and march us all the way to The Station for sodas.

We were just at The Station door when I fell asleep.

I can't say when I awakened. The moon was shining in my opened window, drawing shadows on the wall. My bedposts were the biggest shadows. They rose from floor to ceiling near my door. I imagined they were over-stuffed baseball bats. Now and then they faded with a wisp of a cloud passing over the moon, only to become clear again.

Suddenly the bats disappeared. A new stark shadow blanketed them. It moved from side to side, darkening the room, then letting in light again. As I turned to see what caused it, the shadow disappeared.

Must have been a rain cloud, I thought.

A thump came from outside my window. I opened one eye and spied a mist sweeping past.

"Go to sleep, Billy. You're tired," I told myself.

The thump came again, harder. I opened both eyes. Again the mist swept past.

It was real. I hadn't been dreaming. Someone was outside my window!

"Billyyy. Billyyybeeeeek. Don't be afraaaa-aid. Commmmmm, Billlyyy," called a voice, low and moaning.

I'd heard that voice before.

No. It couldn't be. It couldn't be Old Man Waterman. What was he doing at my house? He belonged at Angel's!

But Angel says he hasn't bothered her, I thought. All this time and he hasn't bothered Angel. Of course. It's me he wants. It was me he wanted on Halloween. Why me? Dear Lord, tell Old Man Waterman to go away!

"Billlyyy. Come heeeere, Billyyy," it moaned again.

Don't panic, I thought. Close your eyes. Make believe you're asleep. But I couldn't.

A white head swished past. Black holes

where eyes should have been. No nose. No
mouth. No body. Oh, horrible white head, go
away. Go away.

The screen rose. The head came in the window — in and out and in and out until I was
sure the sound of my heartbeat would waken
the dead.

The head came into the room. But it wasn't
just a head. It was a head with a body. Arms
and legs moved toward me through the mist!

"Boo!"

Before me stood Angel Wilson, all grins
and happy with herself.

"Scared you. Didn't I?"

I wanted very much to strangle her, and if
it weren't that I'm such a nice kid, I would
have.

"What are *you* doing *here*?" I asked.

She held up some flimsy white material.

"French organdy. Miss Sally'd have a heart
attack if she knew I had it. Pretty good ghost,
huh?"

"Stinks."

I sat up and crossed my legs.

"Baloney. I had you scared to death."

"Don't kid yourself. I was just wondering
who it was."

Angel giggled.

"You were just waiting for Old Man Waterman to gobble you up."

"If you don't keep it down my father will gobble us both up."

It was too late. Just at that moment the door opened.

Between the time my father clicked on the light, and then accustomed his eyes to it, Angel had slipped under my bed.

I covered my eyes, making believe the light was burning them.

"Are you all right, son?" my father asked.

"Yeah. I had a nightmare. I wish you'd turn off that light."

He did, and walked toward my bed.

"I used to have nightmares when I was a kid. Want to talk about it?"

"No. I really can't remember."

"Well, go back to sleep now," he said. "It won't come again."

"I hope not," I said.

He walked toward the door.

"Want me to keep it open?"

"No. I'm okay. Thanks."

He closed the door. I sank back in relief, and waited for the sound of his footsteps to reach his room.

His door opened and closed.

I sat up.

Angel bounced from under my bed.

"Come on," she hissed. "We don't have much time. We have to find the tree. It's the full moon."

"In the middle of the night?"

"Of course the middle of the night. It's more fun. Besides, it's the only time we have without everybody snooping around."

"You find the tree. I'm going to sleep."

I lay back, but she grabbed my arm.

"A partnership is a partnership."

I tried to hug my pillow, but Angel wouldn't let go of my arm. I'd either have to throw her bodily out of the window, or go with her. I decided on the latter. I got up, and threw on some jeans.

I followed her out the window, down from the porch roof to the ground. We sneaked around my house to the back and crossed over to her yard.

Angel's backyard is so big that it could be turned into a country park with land to spare. And she's got enough trees to start a lumber mill. How would we ever find the right one?

The old footpath seemed the best bet. It was the only straight line to any tree, even if it was the dead one in the field.

Sure enough the moon was behind it, just as in the map, and a clear shadow fell in front, pointing to Angel's house.

"If that tree were alive, I'd say this is it," Angel remarked. "Better keep looking."

She wandered to the other side of the yard, but I didn't follow. I wanted time to think, for something was coming to my mind.

It seemed to me that when I was little, the dead tree had been alive. Yes. It had to have been alive then. I remembered that my mother used to paint it. Matter of fact, she won her first prize in an art show for a painting of that tree. Yes. The tree was alive when Old Man Waterman was here.

I found Angel at the opposite corner of the yard, lost in a forest of pine.

"I knew it all along," she said. "I just wanted to be sure. A treasure hunter doesn't take chances."

How about that? I find the tree, and she takes the credit.

Angel pulled a roll of kite string from her pocket. We tied it to the tree and let it out along the shadow. We figured that was the line in the map. The string was almost all used up when we got to the corner of the kitchen.

We looked behind us in dismay. The path was so long that it would take forever to dig for that money.

"If we dug every day for the rest of the summer, we'd never finish," I said.

"Maybe we could rent a backhoe."

"Who'd rent a backhoe to a kid? Anyway, who's got the money for one. I don't."

"I don't either."

We sat on the ground and thought.

"I've got it," Angel exclaimed. "You go home. I'll meet you here at nine o'clock in the morning."

"If you steal a backhoe, count me out," I said. "My father'd murder me."

"We won't need a backhoe," Angel chuckled.

"Then what?"

"You'll see. Be here, nine o'clock sharp."

5

WE DIG

Long before nine the next morning, Tadpole Robertson was at my house, looking as glum as I'd ever seen him.

"What's with you?" I asked, getting him some cereal. "Now that you're starting pitcher, you should be on top of the world."

"That was last night," Tadpole returned, slumping into a chair. "This morning is another story. Jupiter is destroyed."

Jupiter was Tadpole's prize frog, for which he'd paid Bugsy Schmitt a jackknife, five fishing lures, and a dollar. It was a horned toad, very rare for this area, and I'm pretty sure that Bugsy stole it from her father's collection at the college where he is biology professor. At any rate, Tadpole had it in formaldehyde in a giant mayonnaise jar which he kept on his desk. It was the only frog which he didn't keep with the hundred others on the shelves on his wall, and his mother was always warning him that one of these days he was going to break the jar. That's just what happened.

It seems that when Tadpole woke up, he remembered he'd made starting pitcher and got so excited that he grabbed his pitcher's mitt and flung it into the air. The mitt landed on the jar — the jar fell over and smashed.

His father heard the crash, ran to Tadpole's room to see what had happened, got one whiff of the formaldehyde, grabbed the frog from Tadpole, and threw it out the window. The frog landed in the driveway. Before Tadpole could get outside, the baker drove in and squashed it flatter than a pancake.

When Tadpole carried on about it, his father said he was sick of all those creepy frogs anyway.

I'd never seen Tadpole so distraught.

"Bugsy will get you another frog," I consoled.

"Even if she did, it wouldn't be Jupiter," he replied mournfully.

Beats me how anyone could get attached to a dead frog, but Tadpole had. He moped over his cereal. When I offered to make him pancakes, he turned green.

"Reminds me of Jupiter in the driveway," he said.

I felt bad, but it was nearly nine and I had to meet Angel. I decided the best consolation would be distraction.

"You met the new girl?" I asked.

"Nope. My mother got the word on her from Mrs. Jennings. Trouble. Taboo."

"Don't believe it," I said. "Mrs. Jennings is looking for someone to blame because Junior broke his leg. Angel Wilson had nothing to do with it. She's nice. A little crazy, maybe, but nice."

Tadpole raised his eyes.

"Crazy? What makes her crazy?"

"Don't ask," I said, putting my cereal bowl in the sink. "Best you learn for yourself. Come on. I have to meet her. We're looking for Old Man Waterman's million."

Tadpole forgot about Jupiter. He followed me out of the house to Angel's yard. I didn't tell him about the treasure map, and how Angel had scared me near death last night, and how we'd found the path where the treasure was buried. It seemed too complicated.

Angel wasn't in the yard, so we knocked on the door, and Miss Sally let us in.

We followed her to the kitchen where we found Angel munching blueberry muffins. I introduced her to Tadpole and she was pleased to meet him.

"Any friend of Billy's is a friend of mine," she said.

Miss Sally brought us hot muffins, too. While we gobbled them, Angel pulled a batch of flyers from a manila envelope.

"I just finished these," she said. "There ought to be enough."

On the flyer was a picture of a treasure chest with dollar signs all over it. Under the chest was printed the message:

> The area of the Waterman treasure has been located on the Wilson property, but the exact spot is yet to be found. A REWARD of $10,000 IS OFFERED TO THE PERSON WHO LOCATES THE SPOT.
>
> Signed   *Stephen Wilson*
> (*per*) *Angela Wilson*

I asked Angel what "(per) Angela Wilson" meant.

"In the person of, naturally. In reality, this hunt is mine, but since I'm a minor I have to offer the reward in my father's name."

"You mean your father's letting you give away $10,000?" I asked.

"Of course. You have to give a little to get a lot."

Tadpole and I whistled. Our fathers wouldn't part with $10,000 for the world. They'd dig to Africa and back before they'd part with $10,000.

I didn't believe it. I gave Miss Sally a look that asked the question, and she smiled in perfect agreement with Angel. That settled that.

Angel handed me the flyers.

"Here's what you do. Give one of these to each kid you meet, starting with Junior Jennings."

"Junior Jennings!" I said. "After the way his mother bad-mouthed you, you're starting with him?"

Angel frowned. "His mother's suing my father because Junior broke his leg in our tree. We own that field, you know. Anyway, if I make friends with Junior, maybe she won't."

Didn't make sense to me, but then I knew Mrs. Jennings a lot better than Angel did. I took another muffin and Tadpole and I went outside.

"Is it true?" Tadpole asked, pointing to the flyers. "Did she really find it?"

"We both did," I replied.

I showed him the string that led from the corner of the house to the old dead tree.

"It's somewhere along this line."

We started by going across the field to Junior's house, as Angel had directed.

Junior was in his backyard on his crutches, trying to throw a baseball through a tire tied to the tree. His aim was terrible. He missed by three feet.

"Sorry about your accident," I said. "Maybe this will cheer you up."

I handed him the flyer. He read it, whistled, and stared at me. I waited for the nasty remark, but instead he said, "So she's found it. I knew she would," and hobbled toward Angel's yard.

With everyone we met, the reaction was the same — from Bugsy Schmitt, Peter Jenkins, Tony D'Angelo, Wendy Furman, and Mike Callahan. Of the whole mob, not one kid asked a question. Each read the paper, and headed for Angel's.

It was weird. Yesterday they wouldn't talk to her. Today they couldn't get to her house fast enough.

I asked Tadpole what he thought, and he

said, "If she can make a kid break his leg, she can find the treasure."

"But she didn't make Junior break his leg," I sputtered. "He broke it himself. She just happened to be around."

"Maybe she did, and maybe she didn't," he returned, "but for $10,000 I'll take a chance."

After we'd given the flyer to about twenty kids, Tadpole got nervous. He was afraid that if he kept distributing, there wouldn't be a spot left for him in Angel's yard.

"What about you?" he asked.

"I don't need a spot," I boasted. "I get half a million either way. We're partners."

"I'll be darned."

With that, Tadpole gave me his flyers and tore back to Angel's.

I distributed the rest. As I returned, I bumped into kids racing up the street. Bugsy Schmitt stopped long enough to tell me that Angel had let them all stake their claims before she sent them home for shovels.

By the time I arrived at Angel's, the back-yard was a circus. The footpath to the dead tree was marked with English flags ten feet apart. In each section a kid was digging.

A few sections were empty, but as I

watched, kids with shovels scurried to grab them. Between the flags and the kids, it looked like a road gang on parade.

Outside the kitchen stood a long table covered with trays of cookies, and pitchers of lemonade. Miss Sally buzzed in and out with more freshly baked cookies. Any excuse to cook was okay with her.

I asked her where Angel got the English flags, and she told me they'd bought a batch in England after the celebration of the queen's jubilee.

"The queen should see this," I said, and Miss Sally laughed.

There were so many kids I couldn't find Angel. Finally I spotted her coming from the dead tree, all decked out like she was on a safari — with a hat, and jodphurs, and high boots. She had a whistle in her mouth, which which she blew from time to time to give a direction. When she saw me she waved.

"Great dig, huh?"

I didn't have time to answer. A clatter to my left distracted me.

Junior Jennings had fallen. He lay on his back like a turtle, his plastered leg holding him down. I turned him over and helped him to his feet.

"Gee, Junior," I grunted under his weight, "maybe you shouldn't dig, considering your leg."

I thought he was going to cry.

"Please," he said. "It's the first good day I've had all summer. Hand me my shovel."

I gave him his shovel and watched him dig, growing more and more wary as I watched.

The opening at the toes of his cast was filled with dirt. If his mother ever saw that, she'd set the world on fire. And if he ever *really* damaged himself, no telling what she'd do.

Junior had to go. We didn't need the kind of trouble he could bring.

I ran for Angel and pulled her away from the line. No one should hear what I had to say.

"You've got to get rid of Junior. He fell," I said.

"So he fell. He can get up."

"He could not. I had to get him up. You better send him home. He's going to get hurt."

"Baloney. You just don't like him."

"It's not him. It's his mother. There's no telling what she'll do if her precious Junior scratches one little toe in your yard."

When Angel wouldn't listen I reminded her

of what had happened when Junior fell from her tree.

"But Junior really thought I'd hexed him," she explained. "He thinks I have extrasensory powers because of that silly game I was playing. You see, I didn't want to out and out tell him that he stunk at tree climbing. . . . Well, what difference does it make? He thinks I have extrasensory powers and it's the greatest. I told him that he'd be just fine digging where he was, and that his mother would never find him. Poor kid. He's got to get away from her sometime.

"You know what? Maybe I do have extrasensory powers. I sure was smart figuring out that map. I'll be a great treasure hunter."

Angel was impossible. I finally talked her into helping Junior dig. Her extrasensory powers should stay near him, so he wouldn't get hurt.

She gave me her safari hat and whistle, and I set off to check the line of diggers.

What a job. Kids were switching flags and jumping claims. Peter Jenkins and Mike Callahan had such a fight that I had to pour lemonade over them to stop it. Then the flies zeroed in for the lemonade on them, and I had to wash them both down with the garden hose. No problem. It was a hot day and they dried quickly.

At noon, Miss Sally set out a million sandwiches and I blew the lunch whistle.

I got Miss Sally's kitchen timer and told everybody I was setting it for one half hour. When the timer rang they could go back to work, but not a minute before.

While they ate, I reset the flags on the top of the piles of dirt. I didn't want any more riots over claims.

After the gang went back to digging, I ate. I noticed Angel and Junior talking a lot, and wondered what she had to say to a creep like him. I was considering the matter when I spied a well-dressed gentleman with a neat beard coming down the driveway. I ran to meet him.

"Sorry, sir, only kids are allowed to dig. No adults," I said.

The gentleman stared grimly at me.

"Dig for what?" he questioned.

"Dig for treasure."

"What treasure?"

"The Waterman treasure."

The man studied the gang of diggers, then turned to me.

"And who, may I ask, are you?"

"Billy Beak, sir. Partner in the hunt."

"The treasure hunt."

"Yes, sir."

The man gave me the creeps. He asked too many questions.

"Partner with Angela Wilson, I presume," he said.

"Yes, sir."

The man studied the gang again.

"I don't see Angela among this motley crew," he said. "Could you point her out for me?"

I hesitated. Pointing out Angel might be wrong, for the man had a sinister look.

I turned toward Angel and Junior. Evidently they were both sitting in the trench, for I could barely see the tops of their heads. I turned to stall the man when I noticed another person just as sinister coming behind him. It was Mrs. Jennings.

"Hello, Mrs. Jennings," I smiled.

She didn't give me the courtesy of a reply. Instead she turned to the man and said crisply, "Mr. Wilson, I presume?"

"Yes."

I thought I'd choke. He was Angel's father, and he didn't even know about the hunt! Were *we* in for it.

70

Mr. Wilson extended his hand, but Mrs. Jennings refused.

"I am Mrs. Jennings. If you recall, my son broke his leg on your tree. And now I understand he's digging for your treasure."

She pulled one of Angel's flyers from her pocketbook and showed it to Mr. Wilson. When he read it his eyes nearly popped.

Mrs. Jennings continued, "I was considering dropping my lawsuit about your maintenance of a public hazard, mainly the dead tree, but now you can be sure I won't. You can further be sure I will notify the police about your conscription of child labor. People like you belong in jail."

Before I could run to warn Angel, Mr. Wilson had my shoulder.

"Find Mrs. Jennings's son," he commanded, "and get Angel."

6

FIASCO

I ran to Junior's trench and jumped in.

Junior and Angel were crouched like two pretzels in a bean jar trying to keep themselves from view, except, of course that Junior's leg was stretched flat out lengthwise in the trench, giving him more the appearance of a crippled camel with castoff crutches.

From the looks on their faces, I'd have thought that Darth Vader was on the attack.

"Great mess you got us in," I blasted. "Your father knew all about it, huh? And your extrasensory powers were going to keep Junior's mother away."

"Get down. They can see you," Angel hissed.

I squirmed between the two of them.

Angel twisted her neck and peeked over the edge.

"We're lucky. They're so busy arguing they didn't see you."

"What difference does that make? The hunt's over. Your father's going to jail."

"For what?"

"For using kids to dig his treasure. Mrs. Jennings is reporting him. It must be against the law."

"What law?"

"I don't know. Something about conscription of child labor."

She leaned past me.

"Junior, do you really think your mother will report my father?"

"If she's mad enough," he admitted.

"Then we've got to un-mad her. Make her glad again. Think, everybody. Think."

"You think," I growled. "I told you in the first place to keep Junior out of this."

I hurled my safari hat past Junior's open toe.

"Good-bye, million dollars."

"How can you think of money at a time like this?"

"Easy," I said. "I'm a treasure hunter. Remember?"

"Billy, don't you know that there are times when a treasure hunter must forget about his treasure, when he must consider the good of his fellow man? My father is in serious trouble. We've got to get him out of it," Angel said.

She looked again past me at Junior.

"I don't understand why your mother's so mad. We're not digging up *her* yard."

"She thinks it is," Junior replied. "Anyway, she's always mad. If it's not me, it's somebody else."

That was a revelation.

"You, too?" I asked. "She gets mad at you? I thought she thought you were perfect."

"I should be so lucky," Junior sulked.

"Which has nothing to do with saving my father," Angel cut in. "Junior, what's your mother got against him? She's been after him since we moved in."

I knew the answer to that one, but to explain would take too long. Besides, I figured Junior had enough problems. I didn't want to add to them.

"My mother wanted to buy this property," Junior said carefully. "When my father refused she had a fit."

"So that means she has to take it out on *my* father?"

"She'll take it out on anybody. If she catches me here, I'm dead."

I was surprised to hear Junior talk like that about his mother. He never had before.

"Then we'll get you out of here," Angel said protectively. "Billy, stick your head up and see what's happening."

I peeked out and saw Mrs. Jennings waving her hands. Mr. Wilson was facing her. I reported the same.

"Good. We've got a chance," Angel said. "I'll go to them while you get rid of Junior. With any luck we'll save him, and my father, *and* the hunt."

Before I could blink, Angel was out of the trench and running to her father. Slowly she maneuvered him and Mrs. Jennings toward the front of the driveway, out of sight. I knew it was now or never for Junior and me.

"Here's what we do," I said to Junior. "We'll sneak to the trees, and then home. Your mother will never see us through the trees."

"I'll never make it," Junior replied, his head in his hands. "I'm too darn slow on crutches. Angel'd have to keep my mother an hour before I could get home."

I noticed Mike Callahan's bike near the table.

"You won't need the crutches," I said.

"Once we're at the trees I'll put you on a bike and ride you through the field to your house.

"Come on, now. Angel will keep your mother here long enough for you to get home. You know what powers she has."

Good thing Junior was superstitious. When I mentioned Angel's powers his eyes lit up, as if he knew he had a chance.

Although we were only a few feet from the trees, we had a tough time reaching them. For fear his mother might come in sight again, Junior didn't dare walk upright. But he couldn't crawl, so he had to push himself on his stomach.

I held my breath.

He made it. I grabbed his crutches from the trench and got Mike's bike. Junior sat on the suicide bar while I pushed. I couldn't pedal because the ground was so bumpy, and Junior's leg made the bike very heavy, so I had to push.

When we got to his house, I offered to help him clean up, but he said he'd do just fine. He stripped, and I took his clothes back to Miss Sally to wash.

Miss Sally wasn't around, so I went inside and dumped the clothes in the laundry room.

On my way out of the door, Tadpole stopped me.

He wanted another claim. His stunk. It was under the dead tree, and he couldn't get through the roots. I gave him Junior's.

I found Angel with her father, Miss Sally, and Mrs. Jennings in the front of the driveway. They were so engrossed in conversation that they didn't notice my arrival.

"I found Junior," I announced, trying to get Angel's eye, but instead meeting with Mrs. Jennings's, which was snapping.

"Well? Where?" she said. "You've kept me waiting long enough."

"He's home," I replied. "Been there all the time. That's what took me so long. I went clear around the town before I thought to look in his own house. That's where I found him."

"You don't say," Miss Sally smiled. "Well, now, I suppose that proves Angel wasn't lying when she said Junior refused a claim."

Mrs. Jennings didn't reply.

"Gee. Maybe you'll even believe that my father had nothing to do with this treasure hunt. It was all my idea. As I said before, if my father were going to look for the Waterman money, he'd have hired a backhoe," Angel added.

"Exactly," Miss Sally agreed.

Mrs. Jennings didn't look exactly thrilled, but the fire had gone from her eye.

"This whole incident was an unfortunate misunderstanding," Mr. Wilson said soothingly, "but things like that happen with neighbors from time to time. I hope you'll accept our friendship."

We all walked Mrs. Jennings to her car. She said she had to hurry to prepare dessert for the Wednesday Afternoon Ladies Bridge Club. It was only Monday but since it was her turn to host, the dessert had to be special.

"Dessert?" Miss Sally repeated brightly. "Did you say dessert? Dessert. My favorite thing. Now, why should you have to waste this lovely afternoon working on dessert when I have the most marvelous French recipe? Cinnamon chocolate. I won a ribbon for it at Cordon Bleu. Let me make it for you. I insist."

Mrs. Jennings hemmed and hawed, and in the end I wasn't sure whether Miss Sally was or was not making the dessert, but to tell you the truth, I didn't care. I just wanted Mrs. Jennings out of there.

After she'd left we all headed for the diggings, but I held Angel back.

"What did Miss Sally do that for?" I asked.

"You mean the dessert? She was trying to be nice."

"Well, she shouldn't waste her time."

"Why not? If we're nice to Mrs. Jennings, maybe she won't sue my father."

"You don't be nice to rattlesnakes," I said.

"Oh, Billy."

When we reached the dig I forgot about Mrs. Jennings, for the trenches were deep. Any time now someone would hit the million dollars.

"I'm a pretty smart treasure hunter. Aren't I?" Angel said to her father, but he shook his head.

"I don't think a man like Waterman would bury his money where everybody could see him," he said.

"Maybe he did it at night," I said.

Still Mr. Wilson shook his head.

"I'll get my densitometer. We'll see," he said.

Angel groaned, "Oh, no. All my work and he's going to find it. How can I be a treasure hunter if he has all those gadgets?"

I had no idea what a densitometer was, so Angel explained that it was the same as a metal detector, except that it measured the density of elements. She said that soil has a certain density, and that money under it has another one. The different densities would register on the densitometer.

"You mean we could have found the money without all this?" I asked pointing to the mob of diggers.

"That's right."

"Then why didn't we use the densitometer in the first place?"

"It's not as much fun," Angel grinned.

Then she got serious.

"Besides, I had to have a way to meet the kids. It's awful being alone all the time."

Just then, Mr. Wilson came with something like a metal dinner plate on a stick. At the handle of the stick was a gauge which he set for the density of dirt, six feet deep. (We figured Waterman wouldn't have buried the money further than that.)

He explained his machine to everyone. We all followed as he moved it, like a vacuum cleaner, over the trench.

The needle remained steady until we got to Mike Callahan's claim. Then it jumped. Mike and I dug furiously until we hit a boulder.

"I tried to tell you it wasn't money, but you didn't listen," Mr. Wilson said. "The density was too great for money."

Mike groaned, and everybody else sighed in relief.

At the dead tree, the needle jumped all over the place, back and forth, back and forth like a ping pong ball. We were near crazy with excitement until Mr. Wilson explained that the roots of the tree made the densitometer useless.

"If it's here, you'll have to dig to find out," he said.

"No way," Tadpole replied. "The ground is like rock."

"Then you can be fairly certain nothing was buried here," Mr. Wilson said.

Mr. Wilson looked around the field. He could easily see the backyards of the entire neighborhood, for they circled it.

"No," he said definitively "The money isn't buried here. Nobody hides money in a fish-bowl."

We retraced our steps, walking on either side of the trench, moving the densitometer as far as the trees would allow, but nothing registered. Finally we reached the corner of the house.

"I don't know where you got the idea the money was along that path." Mr. Wilson said.

We didn't say a word about the map.

"Try again," Angel cried. "It has to be here."

Once more we walked the trench to the dead tree, moving the densitometer from side to side to get every inch of land. There was no register. I took the machine and walked back.

It was no use. There was no sign of anything buried in the path.

Angel turned to the kids.

"I'm awfully sorry. According to my calculations, the money should have been here, but I was wrong. I'll have to think again."

In a way I was happy. At least the kids knew now that Angel didn't have extrasensory powers. They wouldn't be afraid of her.

But the kids were furious. They grumbled and growled. Mike Callahan asked why we didn't use the dumb machine in the first place.

Angel explained that if she had, there never would have been a contest. Then nobody would have had a chance for the $10,000.

"Nobody had a chance anyway, 'cause it wasn't here," somebody yelled.

"But it was fun looking," Angel replied.

"Some fun."

"Yeah. Great fun."

"Yeah. The blisters on my thumbs are thrilled."

I thought we'd have a mutiny until Bugsy Schmitt came forward.

"I don't know about anybody else, but I had a terrific time. I always wanted to dig up a yard. Really mess it good, but I wouldn't dare touch my own."

We surveyed the wreck we'd made of Angel's yard, and agreed that if we'd done it to our own, it would have been the end. Yes. We'd had a fine time digging that trench, and as long as we didn't have to fill it in, we'd be happy.

"It's not damage a bulldozer can't fix," Mr. Wilson smiled. "I suppose it was worth the fun. Come now, you look like you need refreshment."

"You can keep the flags," Angel offered. "That's the consolation prize."

The kids picked through the dirt for their shovels and English flags. Miss Sally brought out a tank of ice cream. Mr. Wilson followed with cones, and everybody helped himself.

I was too miserable to take any. What a letdown. I'd thought by now that I'd be half a millionaire.

Angel fixed herself a triple dip. She couldn't let a minor setback spoil her appetite.

"Don't worry," she told me. "We'll find the money. I think we read the map wrong. I think we read the map wrong. We must have missed a clue. All we have to do is study the map again and find that clue. That's what my father does when he muffs."

Gradually the kids trickled home, dragging their shovels and flags. Soon it was just Angel, her father, and me in the yard.

"Now you've learned the most important thing about a dig," he said to Angel. "You don't until you've thoroughly researched."

"I did research," Angel protested.

I was waiting for her to tell him about the map, but she didn't, which, when you consider it, was dumb. How was her father to believe we'd researched when we didn't give him any proof?

"No," Mr. Wilson said. "You played games. You guessed, and you guessed wrong. You'd have never done all this work if you'd taken time to consider the man who owned the money. Waterman. What sort of a person was Waterman?"

"What's he got to do with it?" we both questioned.

"Everything," Mr. Wilson replied. "He's the key to the whole mystery. The crux. The missing link.

"Let me explain it to you. Waterman was a miser. Misers don't bury money in the ground. They keep it where they can count it as much as they want. They keep it where they can see it. They keep it where they can be near it all the time.

"You must understand that misers don't just love money, they are obsessed with it. It becomes, in a way, a part of them, so that they and their money can't be separated," explained Mr. Wilson.

"Wow!" Angel said.

"Darn crazy if you ask me," I added.

"So what are you trying to say, Daddy?" Angel asked. "But say it in English this time, 'cause you've been talking five languages at once and I can't understand any one of them."

"What I mean is that if you find Waterman, you'll find his money."

"Ohmygosh."

I could feel my face paling.

"Now that makes sense!" Angel exclaimed. "The only problem is, where can we find him?"

"Who knows?" Mr. Wilson replied. "Frankly, I don't think you ever will. I think the man was murdered."

"Murdered?"

"Murdered. There's a ninety percent chance. You see, he couldn't have disappeared alive without a trace. A person who tries to disappear always leaves clues to his whereabouts behind him."

"But if he was murdered, who did it? And where's the money now?"

"Probably in a foreign country."

My blood was finding its way back to my head. It sure was good to know Old Man Waterman's ghost wasn't floating around Angel's house.

"Baloney," Angel said. "That money's right here and we're going to find it, and I don't want to hear anymore about Waterman being murdered, or disappearing to a foreign country, or anything."

"Well, you're not going to find that money by digging up this yard," Mr. Wilson said, testily.

He strode to the edge of the trench and back again, his arms behind his back.

"Uh oh," Angel whispered, before he'd returned. "He's contemplating. That's dangerous."

Mr. Wilson refolded his arms on his chest and began.

"Angel, I think you're getting carried away with this treasure hunt business. You gave it a try, and had a lot of fun. Now let it go.

"I've got Mrs. Jennings suing me. I've got to put out a fortune to fix the mess you and your friends made. I can't take anymore. I don't want to hear the word 'treasure' again."

Angel opened her mouth to protest, but Mr. Wilson wouldn't wait. He turned and went inside.

For a time neither of us spoke. We studied the long, deep trench which stretched clear to the dead tree, and the piles of dirt around it, scattered with English flags left unclaimed. It was like standing in a littered grandstand after the best game of the year.

Angel put her hand on my arm.

"We've got to find the money, Billy," she said. "My father's going to need it."

7

WE RESEARCH

I'm not certain how Angel arrived at the brilliant deduction that her father needed the Waterman money, and that therefore she had to continue searching for it. It seemed to me that he'd been pretty strong about her deep-sixing the whole treasure idea.

I said as much, but Angel replied, "You don't understand my father. He talks in riddles sometimes. I think he's had to decipher too many hieroglyphics."

I guess I didn't understand her father, but then I didn't understand Angel either. I figured it ran in the family.

I was tempted to ask Miss Sally what she thought about continuing the hunt, but then I knew she'd agree with whatever Angel said. Hadn't she agreed that Angel's father knew that Angel was offering a reward for the treasure?

Considering that, I remembered the tea party and everything Miss Sally said about the balls on the stairs, which brought to mind the thought that the Waterman ghost might just still be around. The whole scheme made me nervous.

After supper that night, I was lying on my bed, deciding whether or not to continue this whacky partnership, when Angel appeared at my window.

If there was one person I did not need around just then it was she. When Angel was around I couldn't think straight. When Angel was around the world was upside down. When Angel was around I found myself lying to the neighbors, sneaking out in the middle of the night, leading a safari of ditch diggers in the backyard, participating in mad tea parties, and refusing free ice cream. Insanity.

I decided not to open the window which was closed — because I never opened it until bed.

On the other hand, Angel had her own ideas. She made sixteen of the most ghoulish faces in captivity, then pounded until I thought she'd bash the window to smithereens. I gave up and let her in.

"Such hospitality," she remarked, climbing through.

Without a "thank you" she strode to my desk, pulled a folded piece of yellow paper from her pocket, unfolded it, grabbed my pen, and wrote,

INVESTIGATION OF OLD MAN WATERMAN on the top line.

"I think we're wasting our time," I said, reading over her shoulder. "We'll never find that money. Whoever murdered Waterman took it."

"Who says Waterman was murdered?" Angel replied. "That's just a supposition. It hasn't been proved. No, there's only one way to find out, if, or if not, he was murdered, and that's by learning more about the man. Isn't that what my father said?"

"Well, yes," I replied, "but — "

"Then it's settled," she cut in, "so we can start our investigation. Now who in town knew more about Waterman than anybody else?"

"Nobody," I said, feeling strangely as if I'd lost a battle I hadn't a chance to begin.

"Nobody?" Angel questioned. "I don't believe it. He had to know somebody. Everybody has to have at least one friend."

"He didn't. Not one."

"Hmm. Our first entry," Angel said. She wrote:

I. FRIENDS.

    A. NONE

    B. NONE

on the paper, and followed it with,

II. BUSINESS ACQUAINTANCES

"Who'd he do business with?" she asked.

"I don't know. The grocer, maybe, but he moved away, and the cleaning lady, but she died. Then there was Tadpole's father. He had something to do with the house, but I don't know what it was."

"Really?" Angel asked, her eyes glimmering. "Do you think he's home now? Do you suppose he'd tell us about Waterman?"

"He's home, all right, but I don't know what he'd tell us. He never talks to Tadpole about it."

"Maybe Tadpole never asked," she said, writing "Tadpole's father" under Roman Numeral II and starring it.

She folded the paper and slid it into her pocket.

"Come on. Let's go and see Mr. Robertson."

Before I'd reached my door, she had the

window open. I decided to climb out with her. It was better that we took the window. That way my parents wouldn't see her going, and wonder how she'd come.

I would have to say something to Angel about her habit of climbing in and out of my bedroom window.

We ran across the street. Tadpole let us in. As I'd expected, his father was in the den reading his paper.

Mr. Robertson is older than my father — anyway, he looks older. His big, thick glasses make pinpoints of his eyes, and I've always found it hard to look directly at them. Actually, I'm a bit afraid of Mr. Robertson. He's much stricter than my father, or should I say he growls a lot more.

When I introduced Angel, she shook his hand, then sat on the couch near his chair.

"I'm here on business," she told him.

"And what business brings you to our home?" Mr. Robertson asked curtly.

"The treasure business," Angel replied, "Waterman's treasure. You see, we're searching for it."

"So I've heard," Mr. Robertson said. "Whatever gave you the idea that the money was along the footpath?"

"It just seemed that way," Angel shrugged. "Dumb, I guess. We've decided to investigate Old Man Waterman. The more we know about him, the better we'll be able to figure where he put his money. And that's why we're here. I understand you did some business with Mr. Waterman, or with his house."

Tadpole and I held our breaths. Mr. Robertson could get pretty nasty when kids asked questions he felt they had no right to ask.

We needn't have bothered. Mr. Robertson smiled quizzically at Angel. We could tell by the glimmer in his pinpoint eyes that we wouldn't have trouble getting information.

"So you want to hear about the Waterman business," he said. "Well, I don't see much harm in it. It's all over now, thank heaven."

He removed his glasses, cleaned them, sighed, put them back on, and began.

"It was the biggest headache I ever had. I don't know why Waterman gave it to us instead of the real estate people. I suppose he trusted us more. We'd done business with him for years. Cashed his bond coupons regularly. Handled his accounts and such. The last time I saw him, he came to the bank to cash in his last million.

"He'd always been nasty, but that day he was abominable. The old vault was on a time lock, and we couldn't get into it until the next morning. I explained that, but Waterman insisted that I drive to the city to get him his cash. I had to oblige. A bank can't let people think it doesn't have money.

"Besides, he made such a row that just to shut him up, Oscar DeGenito told me to go. Remember Oscar?" he said to Tadpole

"Yeah. He was funny," Tadpole said.

"And too soft sometimes," his father replied.

"While I was gone he made a deal with Waterman. In lieu of interest on his deposit, and at a ten-percent-per-expense fee, we would handle all the expenses on his house. He gave us fifty thousand dollars, which in those days should have lasted a long, long time.

"One stipulation was that no one would know about it. Neither Oscar nor any of the bank officers were to tell that they were caretaking the Waterman property — the secret was, when you consider it, impossible to keep, but we tried our best.

"Actually, all we had to do was pay the

taxes and keep people away from the property, plus do a little maintenance here and
there. That seemed easy enough, except that
one month later the police broke into the place.

"I don't know where Waterman was. I
guess he was off spending his money. I tried
to explain that to the police, but they insisted
we post the serial numbers of the million in
cash he'd redeemed. They said they had reason
to believe he'd been robbed and murdered."

"Serial numbers?" I asked.

"Sit down, Billy," Mr. Robertson snapped.
"You make me nervous standing there."

I'd been so interested, I'd forgotten I was
still in the doorway. I sat between Angel and
Tadpole.

Mr. Robertson explained that when a large
amount like a million dollars is issued to one
person, the bank registers the serial numbers.
Then, if it is stolen, the money can be traced.
When the police couldn't find Waterman, every
bank in the country got a copy of those numbers.

"Did they ever show up?" asked.

"Not that I've heard. But there are countries where American currency can be ex-
changed without question. Waterman must
have gone to one of them."

96

"How do you know he went anywhere?" I asked.

"Why would he give the bank money to take care of things if he were staying? In any case, I'm just glad the bank's out of it now. More trouble than it was worth. Everyone wanted to get in the place. Ghost hunters, antique hunters."

"If the bank had the money to pay the taxes, how come we bought the property for back taxes?" Angel asked.

"There wasn't any money left. Two years ago we had to turn the property over to the county.

"Waterman picked the wrong time to disappear. With inflation, expenses tripled. The money soon ran out."

"Then who's haunting his house?" Tadpole asked.

Mr. Robertson laughed, "You don't believe that rubbish, do you? Oh, we got reports of lights in the place from time to time, probably a drifter.

"Angel," he asked, "is someone haunting your house?"

"No," she giggled.

Tadpole and I kept still. What his father didn't know wouldn't hurt us.

Mr. Robertson didn't have more to tell us, so we went to The Station for sodas. I was hoping we'd bump into Jeremiah Cleary, who's generally around there all the time, but we didn't. Jeremiah's the taxi driver, and he knew everything that ever happened in our town.

"What do you think?" Angel asked, sipping a double black and white.

"It doesn't make sense," I replied. "Why would Waterman suddenly hire the bank to pay his taxes if he were going to stay around? He must have gone away."

"I say he was murdered and he's haunting the place," Tadpole said. "Who else bounced that ball down the steps on Halloween?"

When he realized he'd broken our pact, he choked on his sundae. I told him Angel knew what had happened and he was relieved.

"It was one of the thousand balls somebody put on the landing after the police searched the place," Angel said.

She filled Tadpole in on that.

"But who'd put the balls on the steps?" he asked.

"I don't know," Angel said, "Maybe a drifter. Maybe your father was right."

"Maybe he is. Maybe he isn't. There's something crazy about your house. I'm glad I'm not living in it," Tadpole said.

"I've been there over a month and nothing crazy has happened," Angel said. "Ask Miss Sally."

"Don't bother," I cut in. "She makes up better stories than Angel. 'My father knows all about the reward. You have to give a little to get a lot,'" I mimicked. "And then your father comes home and the world caves in."

"Well, if you don't want to believe Miss Sally, ask my father," Angel snickered. "He'll tell you. There's not been a bit of trouble in that house."

"Which means Waterman probably *did* go away, and he took his money with him," I said.

"Well, let's not give up so soon," Angel replied. "Let's keep asking around. It wouldn't hurt. After all, there's a million dollars at stake."

"I don't know," I hesitated.

"If you don't want to be my partner, maybe Tadpole will," Angel said quickly. "Will you, Tadpole, be my partner if Billy cuts out?"

Tadpole's eyes lit up so brightly that I figured I'd better stay with it. After all, I didn't want him to be half a millionaire when I'd had the chance first.

"Okay," I said. "We'll keep looking a little while more."

"I knew you wouldn't let me down," Angel said.

She was pretty, sort of, when she smiled.

We finished our sodas and left.

Mr. Wilson wasn't home, so I couldn't ask him if they'd had any shenanigans with a ghost lately. Anyway, I figured what I didn't know wouldn't hurt me, at least for the time being.

My house was empty. My parents were at the movies. I went right upstairs and threw myself on the bed.

The more I considered it, the more I was convinced that there was a chance the money was still somewhere on Angel's property. It had never shown up in a bank. Even if it was spent in a foreign country, I figured it had to come back to the states sooner or later.

What I didn't understand was how balls could be placed on Angel's landing after the police broke in. True, it could have been a drifter who'd found them and put them there for fun. Then again, maybe Waterman was still around. No, that was impossible. Where was he getting his food? How was he keeping warm in the winter? Surely in eight years' time someone would have seen him.

I was too tired to think anymore. I kicked off my sneakers and crawled under the covers. The next morning I awoke to the sound of tapping at my window.

It was Angel, grinning behind my screen. This business of her popping on and off my porch roof like it was a heliport had to stop.

"Get up," she ordered, opening my screen. "We've a lot to do."

"Do you believe in doors?" I asked.

"Windows are more fun."

"And what do you think my mother would say if she caught you climbing through my window?"

"Good morning, I suppose," Angel returned, plopping on the edge of my bed.

"Wrong. She'd want to know why you sneaked into my room, and what the two of us had in mind. I would be in a bit of trouble, and, in her own words, you would be 'persona non grata' around here."

Angel rolled her eyes.

"That's why I won't have a bedroom. People get too uptight about them. Life would be much better without them."

"Well, I happen to have one, and I wish you'd leave it before my mother finds you."

"Fine."

Angel headed for the door.

"Which way to your kitchen? I'll meet you there."

"Not the door," I choked. "The window."

Angel mumbled something about me making up my mind, but she took to the window.

I got up, closed it behind her, and changed yesterday's clothes, in which I'd slept. As I dressed, I heard the bulldozer filling the trench in Angel's yard.

I went to the bathroom, threw cold water on my face, and brushed my teeth. Then I ran downstairs for breakfast.

My mother and Angel were sitting at the kitchen table, she eating cereal, my mother drinking coffee. I grabbed a bowl from the closet and poured some cereal for myself.

They were discussing Old Man Waterman.

"Rotted vegetables and dented cans of food? Weird!" Angel remarked, screwing her face.

"He was," my mother agreed. "Every Friday morning he'd push a wheelbarrow up the street, park it outside the market, and go inside. On the counter was a supply of dented food cans waiting for him, a nickel apiece.

"He always picked twenty, tapping each can, then shaking it near his ear before he put it in the bag. He'd fish in his coat for a dollar, and hand it over like it was his last.

"He'd take the bag of canned food out to *his* wheelbarrow, then come back for the vegetables. The manager had them set aside for him, too. You should have heard him complain about their condition. I don't know why. He was getting them free."

"What about meat? Didn't he ever buy meat?" Angel asked.

My mother got up and poured herself more coffee.

"No," she said. "Peanuts. He bought a big bag of peanuts. I'd forgotten about that. He put everything in his barrow and went home. Nobody would see him again until the next Friday."

"Did he ever stop to talk on the way?" Angel asked.

My mother sat down.

"Are you kidding? In all the years he lived here, I don't think that man spoke three words to a soul. I tried to be nice to him, but after he screamed at Billy for that ball on his lawn, I stopped."

"He must have talked to somebody," Angel insisted.

"Only when he had to, and that was always business."

"What business?"

"You know, the painter, the gardener, the cleaning lady."

"You mean he spent money on his house?" I asked. "He wouldn't spend money on food, but he spent money on his house?"

"I think he loved that house more than he loved himself," my mother replied. "He certainly took better care of it."

"If he loved the house that much, he'd never have left it," Angel declared. "People don't leave what they love unless they have to."

She made a lot of sense.

"He wouldn't have left his money either," I added.

I felt a little better about sticking with Angel in the hunt. There *was* a chance we'd find the money.

"You mentioned a cleaning lady," Angel said. "Did she ever talk to you? Did she ever tell you anything about him?"

"Mrs. Schmitt?" my mother replied. "She never saw him. He was always in the cellar. She told me that he left her pay on the counter."

Thinking about Bugsy's grandmother made me sad. She'd been dead five years and I still missed her. I used to wait for her every Monday, Wednesday, and Friday afternoon. Five o'clock sharp, she'd leave Waterman's and come past my house.

"Hi, Billy," she'd say. "How's my little man today?"

I could tell her anything, and she'd smile and agree with me. When I dropped her at Bugsy's house, she always gave me candy.

"Where'd Mrs. Schmitt go?" Angel asked.

"To heaven, I guess," I sighed.

Any lady that nice had to go to heaven.

My mother finished her coffee.

"One thing Mrs. Schmitt once told me," she said, putting down her cup, "was that Waterman's kitchen sink was always dirty. She could never figure how one old man could get so much dirt in a sink."

"Probably from cleaning rotten vegetables," Angel groaned.

"No. The sink was dirty three times a week. You'd think it would be just dirty on Fridays if it was from cleaning the vegetables, wouldn't you?"

Who cared. The fact that a man had a dirty sink didn't mean a thing.

"Didn't you hear any stories around town about him?" Angel asked. "There had to be rumors about a person that strange."

My mother never repeats rumors. Bona fide, confirmed gossip, she's only too happy to tell, but never rumors.

Rumors set my mother wild. I think it's because one year there was a rumor that she and my dad were splitting up. It spread like winter flu, and when she heard it, she was spitting mad.

Actually, I think there was some truth to it, because they argued something awful that year. When they weren't arguing, they weren't speaking. I had to carry messages back and forth.

"Billy, tell your mother this."

"Billy, tell your father that."

It was awful. Then one day I came home

from school and asked my mother if she and Dad were getting a divorce.

She nearly flipped. That night she talked to my father for the first time in months. A few weeks later the two of them went off on vacation to the Bahamas, and after that they didn't argue so much. Now they go away every year, while I stay with Tadpole, which I like, except for his frogs.

At any rate, my mother's got this rule about rumors. One should never repeat them.

Frankly, I didn't see how repeating a rumor about Old Man Waterman would hurt, 'cause he wasn't around.

"It's real important, Mom," I said. "Couldn't you break your rule just once?"

"My father says that rules are made to be broken," Angel added.

My mother's face froze. "You don't say?"

Her voice turned sticky smooth. A hint of a smile crossed her mouth, and a glint flashed in her eyes.

That was my mother in a fury. Controlled, but very dangerous. It didn't happen often, but when it did, it was dangerous.

The best thing to do was get lost until she simmered down.

"Uh oh, time to go," I gulped.

Angel didn't take the hint, but I wasn't going to hang around to explain. I went outside and flopped on the chaise, listening to the bulldozer in Angel's yard. She soon followed.

"Your mother says I should ask Mrs. Jennings," she said, sitting on the chaise next to mine. "She says that Mrs. Jennings will tell me any rumor that I want to hear."

"That's my mother's way of socking it to you." I smiled. "If there's one person you don't want to talk to, it's Mrs. Jennings."

"I don't see why," Angel said. "If she knows something we should know, we should ask her about it."

"Believe me, Angel," I said. "You don't want to go to the Jennings's. She's gunning for you."

"Baloney," Angel said. "She's just a little crazy when it comes to Junior. Anyway, what harm can it do to ask her a few questions?"

I tried to convince Angel not to go, but she was determined, so I had to tell her the whole story of Mrs. Jennings.

I was about to begin, when, like a mad bat, Angel took off for the Jennings's house.

"Angel," I called. "Come back. Wait!" but Angel kept running.

What was I to do? I had to go after her. I couldn't let Angel face Mrs. Jennings alone.

"Wait, Angel. Wait for me!" I called.

8

MRS. JENNINGS'S
DESSERT

The backyard at the Jennings's was a shambles, with chairs piled all over the place. Card tables were stacked like dishes in the sink. Rosey, the maid, was opening the tables as fast as she could, with Junior's mother bellowing orders faster than that.

"Put that table to the left. No. The right. No. The left again. Make sure you get it clean, Rosey. Rub hard. Don't forget to rinse."

As she bellowed, she pulled linen napkins from a big box, and folded them next to bunches of silverware on a long table set for a buffet.

Angel watched the scene in amazement.

"What's happening?" she asked me.

"It's her turn for Wednesday Afternoon Ladies Bridge Club," I replied. "Remember she talked about it Monday?"

"Omygosh!" Angel said, "and Miss Sally promised to make the dessert. She forgot all about it!"

She'd no more finished the sentence, when Mrs. Jennings shrieked from across the yard.

"Angel? Angel Wilson . . . Angel Wilson, come here."

"What'll I do?" Angel asked me.

"Run," I said.

"Angel????" Mrs. Jennings called again, speeding toward us.

"I can't run now. She's coming."

"I'll fend her off. You go tell Miss Sally to make the stupid dessert."

"She can't. We don't have the ants."

What ants had to do with it I had no idea, nor did I have time to ask, because Mrs. Jennings was upon us like Gargantua, her beady eyes fixed on Angel.

"Where's that dessert your maid promised me?" she asked.

"The chocolates . . . well . . . yes . . . that's what I came to — "

"She didn't forget them," Mrs. Jennings cut in. "Don't tell me she forgot them, not after all that talk on Monday."

"Well, um . . . uh. Well, you see. . . ."

The best I can describe what happened then is to say that Mrs. Jennings turned into a screaming meemie, waving her arms, huffing and puffing, stamping her feet, carrying on like I've never seen.

"Don't tell me," she howled. "She didn't make them. I can see it in your face. Don't tell me. I can't believe it. Miss Sally didn't make the chocolate dessert. I can't believe it. What am I going to do? What am I *ever* going to do? No dessert for the Wednesday Afternoon Ladies Bridge Club. No dessert! I'll be the talk of the town. I can't believe it. No dessert. In ten years I've never missed dessert. And now because of you. Because of your maid. You did it on purpose. That's what you did. You did it on purpose. You. . . ."

The more she talked the closer her words tumbled on top of each other, so that after a time neither Angel nor I could make head or tail of them.

In her defense, I must explain that hosting the Wednesday Afternoon Ladies Bridge Club and not providing a special dessert is like holding a circus without cotton candy. It's unheard of. Even my mother kills herself on dessert when it's her turn to host.

However, that didn't give Mrs. Jennings the right to throw a fit.

So Miss Sally forgot. Anybody else would get something at the bakery. It might not win a prize, but it would be better than nothing.

But not Mrs. Jennings. She had to be super-perfect-patted-on-the-back all the time, and she couldn't be super-perfect-patted-on-the-back with dessert from the bakery.

If she could have seen herself she might have simmered down. The veins on her temples bulged. So did her eyes. And her face was purple.

"And what is that woman going to do about my dessert?" she shrieked.

Angel shrunk back in terror. She opened her mouth to reply but was tongue-tied. Obviously she wasn't used to anything like this.

I stepped in front of Angel, staring squarely into Mrs. Jennings's bulging eyes.

"That's why we're here," I blurted. "We want to know how many chocolates you need."

"What?" Mrs. Jennings asked, veins throbbing.

"We wanted to know how many chocolates you need. We wouldn't want you to be short dessert for your bridge club."

"We wouldn't?" Angel gasped from behind me.

"No," I said.

"You wouldn't?" Mrs. Jennings questioned.

"We wouldn't," Angel repeated, her voice stronger.

"We wouldn't," I declared sincerely. "You see, we came to ask you about the dessert, but when Angel saw you setting up, she thought you already had dessert, but she didn't want to embarrass you by asking."

"Why didn't she say that in the first place?" Mrs. Jennings asked, her face fading to red.

"I stutter sometimes," Angel explained.

"A likely story," Mrs. Jennings said.

"It's true!" Angel declared, fully recovered from her case of tied tongue.

I found her toe behind me and crunched it. The less she said the better. She pulled it from under my heel and kicked me.

"If you haven't yet begun to make the chocolates, how will you be able to finish them on time?" Mrs. Jennings asked. "Bridge starts at one."

"They don't take long," I replied.

Never having made chocolates, I had no idea how long they took, but it was the best answer.

"Hmmm," Mrs. Jennings said. "Are they large?"

Her voice was now its ordinary treble, her face normal—sallow with rouge.

"Not very," Angel replied, coming next to me, "but rich. You know how French confections are."

"Of course," Mrs. Jennings said.

I doubted she'd had French candy in all her life, for she wasn't exactly a world traveler. Mr. Jennings went away a lot, but he never took his wife.

"Tell Miss Sally I'll need a hundred," she said at last.

"A hundred," I repeated. "Don't worry. You'll have them. Let's go, Angel."

We couldn't get out of there fast enough.

Halfway across the field I stopped running, so that Angel could catch up.

" 'Bout time you slowed down. My toe is killing me. You should have stepped on her toe, the old bag."

"In this town, one doesn't step on Mrs. Jennings's toe," I said.

"Maybe *one* doesn't, but *I* do," she replied, tossing her head. "At least I'd like to. Who is she anyway? The empress?"

No, she wasn't the empress, and nobody much liked her, for she had an iron tongue. But she was the lady who'd gotten us the Little League Field, a new auditorium in the school, started the bridge club, and ran the PTA and the Greater Shore Area Antique Show which made a lot of money for the Sports Association. She did all the work that nobody else wanted to do, so she had a right, sort of, to be a witch.

Angel didn't buy it.

"Nobody has the right to be that nasty."

I further explained that the Wednesday Afternoon Ladies Bridge Club had a weekly contest over the dessert, and that if Mrs. Jennings didn't serve a nice one today, she'd be the talk of the town.

"Serves her right. If she thinks that Miss Sally and I are going to tear this town apart looking for ants for chocolates, she's crazy."

Ants? What ants?

"*Cinnamon* ants," Angel said. "They taste kind of sweet and spicy in one. You mix a bunch with sugar and chocolate and nuts. Miss Sally has the recipe. Mmm, delicious."

"You mean real ants?"

"What other kind are there? Don't tell me you never heard of cinnamon chocolate. How provincial."

I'd just as soon be provincial as eat ants. What kind of a screwball ate ants?

"We had them in Paris," Angel explained dreamily. "They're seedy to crunch on, like granola cookies. I'll have Miss Sally cook you a bunch someday."

"Yech. No, thanks. Good thing you're not making them for Mrs. Jennings either. If the ladies ever knew she'd serve them ants. . . ."

"You don't say? Well, now. That changes everything."

The gleam in Angel's eye told me her mind. If I could get the ants — which wouldn't be hard — Bugsy's father had gobs of them at the college — we would help Miss Sally make the chocolates for Mrs. Jennings.

Naturally we wouldn't divulge the recipe. Instead, Angel would wait for Mrs. Jennings to ask. Then Angel would publish the recipe in the *News* under the title "Mrs. Jennings's Chocolate Surprise."

"But you have to make sure you get *cinnamon* ants," Angel said. "Nothing else tastes as good."

"How can I tell?"

"I don't know. Get red ones. They must be cinnamon."

I hopped on my bike and headed for Bugsy's, while Angel raced home.

I caught Bugsy on her way to the beach and explained the situation.

"I don't know," she hedged. "My father still hasn't recovered from his horned toad."

"How much do you want?" I asked.

Bugsy was a mercenary. Wiggle a dollar under her nose, and she'd steal anything.

She thought a moment, then smiled her own, sweet dollar-sign smile.

"Two thousand dollars."

Two thousand dollars? Was she crazy? Where were we to get two thousand dollars? Why didn't she ask for a million?

The more I protested the wider she smiled. Finally, when I was worn out she said sweetly, "I don't know what you're so uptight about. I don't want it right away. I can wait until you and Angel find Waterman's million."

"But I'm not sure we'll find Waterman's million. I'm not even sure there is a million. What will you do if we don't find it?"

"Tell you what," Bugsy said. "If you find it, you owe me two thousand dollars. If you don't,

I'll settle for five dollars and Angel's safari hat. Either way, I'll give you until the end of summer — September 1."

I didn't care about Angel's hat, but thought five dollars was a little much for a bunch of ants. However, Bugsy was adamant. She wouldn't shave a nickel from her price.

"Take it or leave it," she said.

"I suppose I'll have to take it," I replied.

After all, what good were chocolate ants without the ants?

Like all mercenary creatures, Bugsy just happened to have paper and pencil on her, and I signed the IOU. Then she turned her bike around, and we headed for the college.

We parked in the back of the science building, and sneaked in through the basement. Summer classes were on, but luckily no one was in the entomology lab.

"Nobody studies bugs," Bugsy grimaced. "You can't make a living with them."

I didn't reply. I knew that Bugsy's father had a tough time making ends meet on his salary as a professor. Maybe that's why she was such a mercenary.

The lab was loaded with ants, all colors and sizes, each species living in its own glass tank labeled in Latin.

There were a number of red ants, and we couldn't decide which would be best. We sniffed at air holes until we found a tank that smelled like cinnamon. We pulled that out, and arranged the remaining tanks so that no one would notice the empty space.

To camouflage the tank we covered it with Bugsy's beach towel.

I'd never realized how heavy a tank of ants could be. By the time we got to our bikes, we were huffing like mountain climbers.

The tank was so heavy it squashed Bugsy's basket (for which she was going to charge me, but I said there was nothing in the IOU about damage to her property, after which she was going to bring the ants back, but she couldn't carry them alone, so she had to give in), so I balanced the tank on my suicide bar and walked the bike.

If you have ever walked a tank of ants a mile on a bicycle, you will understand when I tell you that by the time we reached Angel's, my arms were killing me.

"What took you so long?" Angel asked impatiently.

I could have dumped the ants on her head and laughed gleefully while they crawled all over her, but my arm ached too much.

Her part of the contract fulfilled, Bugsy left for the beach.

Angel and Miss Sally brought the tank inside. I'd worked enough.

While I rubbed my sore arms, they set the tank on the counter near the sink and began spooning dirt and ants through a sifter. When the sifter was full, Angel put it under the faucet, washing the dirt down the drain, while stirring the ants so they'd be clean.

Miss Sally stirred a vat of chocolate bubbling on the stove.

"Hurry, before the chocolate burns," she urged.

Sifter after sifter of sparkling clean red ants were dumped into the chocolate. Pretty soon the vat was crawling with them. What a way to die.

After all the ants had been emptied into the vat, Miss Sally gave one last stir and lifted it from the stove. Carefully she poured the mixture into eight rectangular cake pans.

"I hope we can save a few for ourselves," she said, scraping the vat. "It's a shame to do all this work and not get anything from it."

"Me, too," Angel agreed, licking her lips.

Yech.

Angel looked at me and grinned.

"Don't knock it till you've tried it," she said.

"I'll take your word it's good," I replied.

We put the pans in the freezer so they'd cool faster, and while Miss Sally cleaned the mess, we ate an enormous lunch of cheese and blueberry pie.

How I could eat after making chocolate ant candy I don't know, except that now that it was in the freezer I didn't have to think about it. Besides, the smell of chocolate in the kitchen made my mouth water.

Angel wasn't nearly as hungry as I. She let me finish the pie, while she helped Miss Sally cut the chocolate, and what a cutting that turned out to be.

Diamonds, hearts, clubs, and spades, all cut from each pan like the chocolate was cookie dough. I don't know how many hundred there were, but when she was finished Miss Sally had ten round platters all arranged in circles of alternating suits. In the center of each platter she placed a crab apple and shoots of mint.

It sure looked delicious. If I didn't know what the chocolate was made of, I'd have grabbed a platter for myself.

Angel took a handful of crumbs from a pan. "Mmmm. Try some."

I declined, but Miss Sally helped herself.

"I think it's better homemade," she smiled. "It always is."

Angel nodded and picked a heart from the edge of one of the platters, grinning impishly at Miss Sally.

"Don't worry," Miss Sally chuckled. "We won't give them all to that Jennings creature. We'll keep two plates for ourselves."

Angel popped the heart into her mouth.

I was sorry I'd been so hoggish about the pie, for my stomach'd begun to churn. I concentrated on the ceiling while Angel and Miss Sally devoured one whole platter of chocolate ants and every crumb in every pan.

It was time to go.

We each took four platters, covered them with aluminum foil, and placed them gingerly on huge trays.

"Be careful," Miss Sally warned, as she opened the door. "Don't run. You'll spill them."

Once free of the kitchen my stomach settled.

We walked slowly through the field. Halfway across I spotted Mrs. Jennings waiting for us at the edge of her yard.

"Wait till she tastes these," Angel bragged.

Mrs. Jennings was in her usual state of fury, except that her temples weren't bulging so badly.

"About time," she snapped. "I was beginning to wonder if you were coming."

"Open a platter and try one," Angel grinned.

Mrs. Jennings undid the aluminum, bit into a chocolate, smiled, and blinked.

Funny. As I watched her chew, my stomach felt great.

"Maaaarvelous!" she exclaimed, with enough "thank you's" and "but you really shouldn't have's" to set a record.

"You'll win a prize for these," Angel giggled, and Mrs. Jennings heaved a sigh of glory.

We were placing the chocolates on the table, when Junior hobbled from nowhere for a piece.

"Not bad," he remarked.

"Junior, don't touch them," his mother shrieked.

As Junior slunk away, Angel watched him, grimly shaking her head.

"He doesn't have a chance," she said.

Luckily Mrs. Jennings didn't hear. She was busy with the ladies arriving for bridge. Like Miss Piggy, she flitted from one to the other.

When I saw my mother, I considered warning her about the dessert, but decided against it. She didn't eat chocolate.

No sense hanging around. We might look suspicious.

Angel and I raced to my yard. I won and threw myself on the grass, rolling with laughter until I couldn't breathe.

What a trick. What a day. Angel and I had put one over on Iron Tongue Jennings. Beautiful, beautiful day.

We sat up, looked at each other, and broke into more laughter. Finally, exhausted, I lay back panting.

"We did it!" Angel sang.

"We sure did! Hey!" I sat up. "Let's go to the beach."

It was a beautiful day for it.

Angel sat up also and eyed me, her mussed-up blond hair sprinkled with green grass.

I realized that it was the first time I'd directly asked her to go with me. I'd always said I'd meet her down there, but never go with her.

"Naw," she grinned. "We lost too much time already. Let's track those rumors down."

I knew she was glad I'd asked.

Angel was right. A good treasure hunter kept going, even if it meant he'd miss a perfect afternoon at the beach. I'd take her to see Jeremiah Cleary. He knew everything about everybody.

9

JEREMIAH CLEARY'S
STORY

We found Jeremiah Cleary puffing his pipe and sitting next to Petunia, his taxi. Petunia was a genuine 1937 black Cadillac limousine, long and fancy, with chrome and running boards, which Jeremiah kept spit polished and tuned to a purr. My mother says that Jeremiah never married because he was too much in love with Petunia.

I suppose I have a weird town — Old Man Waterman in love with his house, Jeremiah Cleary in love with his taxi.

Jeremiah was sitting where he always sat, at the train station, waiting for the Afternoon Special, which was a local with four cars. He always got a crowd from the Afternoon Special, for kids from the neighboring towns were always having birthdays.

The best birthday present in the world to any outsider under eight years old was a trip on the train to Jeremiah Cleary's spit-polish-gleaming old-fashioned Cadillac limousine, a drive in the limousine while Jeremiah announced to all the CB world that Spunky Spoon or Sally Snod was taking her birthday jaunt, an ice cream soda at The Station, and the train back home. Sometimes a mother got Jeremiah to drive her kid home, but that cost, 'cause Jeremiah was no dunce when it came to money.

I never understood what was so special about a ride in Petunia, but then, I could ride her anytime. When I was little, Jeremiah used to take me in the front seat with him. He doesn't anymore, although he'd like to.

He asks me all the time, "Billy Boy, when are you coming out with me and Petunia?"

It's hard to tell a man you're too old for the most important thing in his life.

"Ho, now, Billy Boy," Jeremiah called, taking the pipe from his mouth. "I bet you want to introduce your little friend to Petunia."

For as long as I can remember Jeremiah has called me Billy Boy. I hate it.

"Yes, I do," I replied, "and to you, too."

"Angel Wilson, this is Jeremiah Cleary and Petunia."

Angel nodded to Jeremiah and looked around.

"Where's Petunia?" she asked.

Jeremiah threw back his head and laughed, exposing teeth browned from pipe tobacco.

"Watch or she'll run you over," he said, pointing to the taxi. "Billy Boy, I'm surprised at you. Shame."

"Gosh," Angel said. "I never guessed your taxi was as nice as this. The only ones I've ever seen are yellow, with signs on top."

She opened Petunia's door and ran her hand over the upholstery.

"How do you keep her so nice?"

Jeremiah glowed. There was nothing so wonderful as someone's making a fuss over his Petunia. He got up and went to her, patting her chrome headlight.

"I take good care of Petunia," he said. "Tune her every week. Shine her every morning. She's old, but better than new.

"Most people dump a car when it's old, and that's a shame, 'cause a lot of fine machines have gone to the yards. Course nowadays it doesn't make much difference. They make cars so they'll fall apart. Petunia here, she's different. She comes from the old days. She was made to last."

"I guess she was," Angel said, shutting the door and walking around to view all her sides. "What a beauty. I'll bet she's worth a lot. My father says the older a thing, the more it's worth."

"I've been offered a fortune for her," Jeremiah boasted, "but I wouldn't part with Petunia for all the money in the world. We've been through too much together."

I should have known! Jeremiah was going to tell the saga of his life with Petunia, and Angel was going to let him.

Jeremiah returned to his chair and relit his pipe, while Angel leaned against Petunia and waited. I glowered at her, but she made believe she didn't see.

"It was Seeley's limousine," he started, "almost new when they lost their money in the Depression." He looked at Angel. "You're too young to know about those days."

"I've read about them," Angel replied.

"It's not the same as living them," Jeremiah returned, staring at the air as if searching for something in it.

"Bad times. Really bad. I was Seeley's

chauffeur until he couldn't afford to pay me. Then I drove the family around for nothing until I'd worked enough to earn the car. Best day of my life was the day Mr. Seeley signed Petunia over to me.

"I started a taxi business to pay for her gas, but it was tough. Nobody had money for a cab. I was about to give up when Mr. Waterman came to town.

"He came to see Mr. Seeley, on business, I figured, 'cause he carried one of those fancy leather briefcases. I don't know what his business was about, but right after he left, Mr. Seeley jumped off the roof of his house and landed in a tree.

"Snapped his neck and just about every other bone in his body. It took them hours to get him down. Had to send for one of those city fire trucks with high ladders, and when they reached him, they had to cut the branches away to get him out.

"I can still see his body as they lowered it on a rope, broken bones jiggling. His head was swelled like a martian — his face all purple with eyes popping out, staring wherever the head bobbed. His jaw hung open like it wasn't part of his face. His tongue was blue."

"Yech," Angel grimaced.

I'd heard the story so many times before that it didn't faze me. However, Jeremiah paused until I'd made a suitably sickened face. Then he continued.

"After that, people kept coming to town to see the Seeley estate. Got to be a regular tourist attraction. Ghoul hunters, I called them, although it gave me business for Petunia.

"Then word got out that before he'd died, Seeley had sold his estate to a man named Waterman. The folks at Town Hall said he'd given it away, the price was so low."

"You're not talking about Old Man Waterman, are you?" Angel interrupted.

"There was only one," Jeremiah replied. "I'll tell you about him next. One thing at a time."

Jeremiah continued. Once he started a story he didn't stop for anything.

"Seeley's widow had an auction to sell off her furniture. It was like a county fair. Folks from miles around swarmed in like buzzards. People sold popcorn and ice cream, and everything else you could think of. One man even sold pictures of Seeley's body being lowered from the suicide tree. Lord!

"That morning Petunia and I were the busiest we'd ever been, carting mobs from the train. Then I closed shop to watch the auction.

"Never did like Seeley's wife, or their daughter for that matter. Snobs, they were, but when I saw them that day I felt sorry for them. They stood near the auctioneer, Mrs. Seeley clutching that girl of hers, watching her beautiful furniture go for nothing. Cheap crowd, or maybe just poor. Times were tough.

"Strange lady, Mrs. Seeley. The only money she had coming to her was what she could make on the auction, but she wouldn't sell her silver, although it was worth a fortune — coffee services, and tea services, and plates, and dinnerware. Said her little girl was going to get it. And that girl was determined to see that she did. She kept one hand in her mother's and the other on the crate holding the silver. If anyone came near the crate she blasted him. What a mouth.

"The auction hadn't been going long, when Mr. Waterman came. I recognized him right away as the man who came to see Seeley before he died. It wasn't until he outbid everybody on the rest of the furnishings (though not by much), and had them put back into the house that I realized he was the new owner.

"Everyone else must have figured the same, for they all went up and introduced themselves. My, he enjoyed it. He wasn't friendly, mind you, more like a new-crowned king, but I could tell he loved every bow that came his way.

"He didn't once look toward Mrs. Seeley or her girl. Although they weren't ten feet from him, he never let on he knew they were there.

"Knowing the Seeley girl, I expected she'd walk right over and give him a piece of her mind, but she didn't. Instead she came to me. (I wasn't far — just under the suicide tree.)

" 'Jeremiah,' she commands, like she was still princess of her estate (like I was a piece of dirt), 'I'll expect you to take us to the station. It's the least you can do since you've stolen our car.'

"I was surprised. If anyone had stolen anything, Waterman had stolen her estate. And I *hadn't* stolen her car. I explained that

I'd earned the car, but she wouldn't listen, kept stamping her foot and yelling I was a thief. The more I talked, the madder she got. Didn't make sense at all.

"I killed her father. I stole her house. I stole her car.

"Terrible. Everyone was looking, except for Mr. Waterman, who'd finished his receiving line and gone into the house. Mrs. Seeley tried to calm her daughter, but that was impossible.

"Just to get them away (and me too), I drove them to the station. That girl screamed at me the whole time.

"I was plenty relieved when the train pulled out with her on it. I figured I'd seen the last of that girl, but twenty years later she came back, all grown and married, but not any nicer. She's been screaming at the town ever since, and when she sees me she near pops her cork!

"I'm surprised that when the Waterman place went up for sale, she didn't get her husband to buy it, to reclaim her old home. Then maybe she'd be happy. But she didn't. I suppose she'll go on being mad for the rest of her life.

135

"Lord. That Harriet Jennings is something. Miss Harriet. One of these days she's going to bust a blood vessel with that disposition of hers."

"Jennings?" Angel said. "Harriet Jennings? Do you mean the Seeley girl is Mrs. Jennings?"

"Didn't you know? Didn't Billy Boy tell you?"

"Billy Boy didn't tell me a thing!"

Angel's face was a cross between shock and fury, a bit tilted toward the fury.

"Why didn't you tell me, Billy? You should have told me," she exclaimed.

"At first I forgot about it," I said. "Then this morning I tried, but you didn't give me a chance. You were too set on going to the Jennings's. You ran away so fast I couldn't catch up with you."

"But it was so important," Angel said. "That's the whole reason Mrs. Jennings is giving my family a hard time. We're living in her house!"

"It isn't her house. It's yours," I said. "Anyway, even if you hadn't bought her house, she'd give you a hard time. That's the way she is."

Jeremiah agreed.

"Some people are born nasty and she's one of them," he said. "I know. I was there long before her father had his troubles. If she still owned that house she'd probably be worse than she is, be pouncing around here like a bella donna."

I think Jeremiah meant prima donna. Then again, bella donna fit Mrs. Jennings better.

"But Billy should have told me," Angel said. "At least I'd know what her problem was. It must have been awful for her, her father dying, then her house sold out from under her."

"Don't worry your pretty head about it," Jeremiah said. "Lots of people have terrible things happen to them, but they don't wind up the witch she is. They hurt, but they learn to handle it."

He changed the subject.

"Now, what's this about Mrs. Jennings giving you a hard time? Anything I haven't heard already?"

It was Jeremiah's way of exchanging one good story for another, but Angel didn't know that.

"Nothing I can't handle," she replied absently.

Evidently her mind was still on Mrs. Jennings.

"Did Jimbo Micklewitz ever call your father?" Jeremiah continued. "Harriet Jennings nearly shrunk his ears over the fact you had the kids digging for Waterman's money, but Jimbo told her he couldn't do a thing about it. There's no law against offering a reward.

"Jennings said it was a disgrace that all those kids were working in the sun, said he ought to get down there before someone died of sunstroke."

Jimbo is our police chief. I wasn't sure Angel knew that, but she did. And when she heard Jeremiah, she snapped back to the present mighty fast.

"I didn't know she'd called the police. She promised she wouldn't. Darn! You're right. Here I was feeling sorry for her when she's nothing but an old witch. I can't believe it. I'm feeling sorry for her after she had the nerve to call the police on my father.

"I knew I shouldn't have made that dessert for her. I should have let the Wednesday Afternoon Ladies Bridge Club do without dessert and talk about her all night. That's what I should have done. Darn!"

"That's why you made the dessert. Remember?" I chuckled. "Don't worry. They'll talk about her plenty after they see the recipe."

"You're right!" Angel chuckled with me. "I'd forgot all about it."

Jeremiah knew nothing about Angel's chocolate ants, so we told him. Angel didn't know it, but she was getting her revenge on Mrs. Jennings sooner than she'd planned, for the first chance he had, Jeremiah would blab to his CB friends.

Jeremiah thought it was the best trick he'd heard. He slapped me on the back until my ribs vibrated. He told Angel she was the spunkiest kid he'd met. We were so proud of ourselves that we almost forgot the reason we'd come. It wasn't until he brought it up that we remembered.

"You never found Waterman's million yesterday, did you?" (As if he didn't know.)

"No," I replied.

"Of course not. He never buried it. He liked money too much to put it in the ground, unless he could be with it."

"That's what Angel's father said," I replied.

"And I suppose he told you that you'd have to learn more about the man before you could find his money," he said.

Jeremiah was smarter than I thought.

"Well, I like you, and I'd like to see you find that treasure, if for no other reason than to show up that Jennings woman, so I'm going to tell you what I know."

Even if he didn't like us, Jeremiah would have told us what he knew, 'cause Jeremiah loved to talk.

Angel and I sat on the stoop. Jeremiah banged the dead tobacco from his pipe, put in fresh from his pouch, and lit it. After a few puffs, he began.

"He was jilted. That's what he was, jilted, forty years ago, and I can't blame the lady who did it. A mean one, he was, and she was sweet. Oh, he was dapper in those days, a regular dandy. Always wore a silk suit and a panama hat. You could tell by the way he swaggered that he thought he was fine. I never liked him though. Cheap, even then.

"The first time he got off that train he made me drive him to the Seeley estate for fifteen cents. Fifteen cents barely covered Petunia's gas, but I needed the money, and he knew it.

140

"I always felt he had something to do with Seeley's committing suicide. Why would Seeley sign that beautiful estate over to him for nothing unless Waterman had something on him? Even in those days the estate would have brought plenty."

Jeremiah's pipe had gone out, so he lit it again.

"Now, where was I? Oh, yes. He was jilted.

"After the Seeleys moved, Waterman had the house remodeled. He spent a fortune. Best thing that happened in the town, 'cause people needed the work.

"One day he came to town with a beautiful young lady, sweetest face I've ever seen. A lot like what yours will be when you grow up, Angel."

Angel smiled.

"Naturally he got me and Petunia to drive them around town, and then to the estate. He told his lady that I was his chauffeur, but I fixed him for that, and for gypping me on my fares, too. When I opened the door to let him out I asked for my pay."

Jeremiah chuckled.

"I said he owed me two weeks, forty dollars.

"He was trying to make an impression on the lady. When I said that, his face turned scarlet.

"The lady thought it was funny.

" 'Pay the man, John,' she says.

"So he paid me, but he wasn't happy about it. Said he'd get me back, but he never did, really, 'cause business started to pick up, and I didn't need his fifteen-cent fares anymore.

"Waterman took the lady around the estate, and then I drove them back to the station. There was time to kill before the train, so they sat in the back of Petunia, talking. That's when I heard them planning their honeymoon — arguing, I should say. She wanted Europe. He said no.

"When the train came, she told me I was a fine chauffeur, and she'd be pleased to have me in her employment after the wedding. I din't tell her that I wasn't her chauffeur. I figured I'd wait until the time came.

"A few weeks later, Bert, the stationmaster, showed me a newspaper with the lady's picture in it. She'd married a Frenchman.

"A month passed. One day Waterman came on the train. He was alone, carrying two satchels. He told me I owed him a ride to the estate, which I did, I suppose. When we got there, he told me not to wait. A few days later his trunk arrived.

"For years he went back and forth to the city every day. I drove him to and from the station for my regular fee, fifty cents, take it or leave it. Course, in time I raised that.

"You'd think that after a while we'd have gotten friendly, but he never talked. At first I thought it was because I'd tricked him out of forty dollars, but then I learned he never spoke to anyone.

"After the war the price of property went sky high, and he sold off most of the estate, just kept what you have now, Angel.

"He made a million dollars on the land. I know, 'cause the developer told me what he paid. That's what you kids are looking for, the money he made on the land. I guess he didn't need to work after that; he stopped going to the city. Stayed in his house all the time.

"That's when he let himself go. Never got a haircut or shaved, wore anything he could get at the second-hand store."

Jeremiah puffed on his pipe. It had long since gone out, so he relit it.

I heard the whistle of the Afternoon Special, and knew that soon he would be too busy to talk to us.

"Don't you know anything else?" I asked. "Did he have friends from the city? Did anyone come to visit him?"

"Not one."

"What about his house? When they remodeled it, did they put in a secret room?"

I don't know why I asked that. I guess I was looking for someplace Old Man Waterman could hide while the police searched his house.

Jeremiah puffed.

"So far as I know, the only structural change in the house was a new kitchen upstairs. The old one had been in the basement. I don't recall anyone telling me about a secret room."

He puffed on his pipe some more.

"Have you checked the plans?" he asked. "I mean, compared the Seeley plans to the ones Waterman made when he remodeled? I think what you're looking for would be in the Seeley plans."

Plans. We'd never thought to look for plans.

"I've never seen plans," Angel said.

Jeremiah continued as if she hadn't spoken.

"I doubt if there is anything like a room, though. I worked for the Seeleys a long time, and never heard of one. Then again. . . ."

He stopped.

"Well?" Angel asked.

"I've heard that Mr. Seeley's grandfather was a strange one. He did his business in a guest house in the field, but no one ever saw him coming to or going from it. Maybe it's a tunnel you're looking for."

"A tunnel," Angel said. "Would that be in the plans?"

"Try to find them," Jeremiah smiled. "If it's a tunnel, it's in the old plans. If it's a secret room, it's in the new."

The Afternoon Special pulled in. Twenty kids piled out, followed by their mamas. Jeremiah banged the tobacco from his pipe and put it in his pocket.

"Sorry I can't help you anymore," he said, as he headed for Petunia.

"You helped a lot. Thanks," Angel returned. "We'd never have thought to look for the plans if we hadn't talked to you."

Jeremiah stopped.

"Well, then, I'll do one thing more. Heh. Heh. I'll publish your story about the chocolate ants. Chocolate ants for the Wednesday Afternoon Ladies Bridge Club. Heh. Heh. Harriet Jennings will have a bird."

Jeremiah started Petunia with her first load of birthday kids. He took the CB mike in his hand.

"Mrs. Jennings's Chocolate Surprise," he called with a wink as he passed us.

Tonight the word would be out on Angel's dessert. The town would be buzzing.

We didn't know it then, but those chocolate ants would save our lives.

10

WE SEARCH

Our research was over. We had something
to go on. There might be a secret room or a
tunnel in Angel's house. The money might be
in there.

What had happened to Waterman we didn't
know, but we were too excited about the
prospects of finding the money to worry
about him.

Instead of killing ourselves looking for a
secret room or tunnel, we decided to do what
Jeremiah suggested and find the plans to the
house. They'd save us a lot of trouble in the
long run.

Angel'd been pretty much through the
whole house, and she remembered seeing lots
of papers in the attic, so we started there.

It was hot as a boiler. We opened as many
windows as we could, but they didn't much
help, for there was little breeze outside that

day. The little that brushed through scattered the dust so that it choked us.

A hundred years of dust clung to the boxes, and chests cluttered helter-skelter throughout the attic. It was thick as a carpet, and what didn't choke us stuck to our sweating bodies, so that we were soon smeared with it.

"Let's hurry and get out of here," I said, wiping the perspiration from my eyes.

No time to consider the heat. Too many boxes to open, dresser drawers to pull, documents to scan, old clothes to muddle through.

We opened a box packed with small bright feathers that curled. Another held never-used silk. There were blankets and bedspreads sealed in mothballs, disintegrated with age.

In a desk we found a packet of letters which told us that the Seeley family made its fortune gun-running for the South during the Civil War.

"Look at these orders," Angel said, showing me one for fifty crates of rifles. "Where could Seeley have hidden all those guns? There has to be a secret room."

"I guess so," I replied, "but wherever it is, it sure is secret. Even Jeremiah didn't know about it and he lived here."

"Maybe it got sealed off after the Civil War. Maybe Seeley's grandfather never told anybody about it."

"He could have been more helpful."

"Doesn't seem anybody who lived in this house was ever much help."

We put the orders down and went on.

We learned that Mr. Seeley, who had died in the tree, had owned an accounting firm, for in a huge carton was stationery with his letterhead on it.

"Why would a person who has his own company kill himself?" I asked.

"We'll worry about that after we find those plans," Angel replied.

She was right. We were uncovering so many puzzles attached to this house, that if we stopped to figure them all, we'd never find a thing.

We ripped the place stem to stern but didn't find the plans.

"A lot of good that did," Angel said, disgustedly, wiping the perspiration from her dust-streaked face. "The only thing we did was wreck the place. Good thing Miss Sally doesn't come up here or she'd have a fit."

We certainly had made a mess. I don't

think the Huns, Vandals, Goths, and Visigoths did as bad a job on Rome.

No plans in that attic. We closed the windows and headed downstairs. At the third floor, where there was air conditioning, I took my first deep breath in over an hour. Sure felt good.

"Where next?" I asked.

"The second-floor bedrooms. I never got to check them through. Miss Sally was always in the way."

We swung down to the second floor, which was pretty much like the third, except that the halls were wider.

Like everything else in Angel's house, the bedrooms were huge. But not one of them contained a closet. Instead, they held wooden monstrosities which Angel called chifferobes. One side of a chifferobe contained drawers, top to bottom; the other held a crosspole on which clothes were hung. Great doors with brass handles hung in the front.

I thought the chifferobe the ugliest furniture I'd seen. It seemed to me that Angel's father would be a lot smarter if he burnt them all for firewood and built closets in the space they took.

We took the first room off the back stairs and started with the chifferobe. We pulled out every drawer, then banged the back of the closet part to see if it was solid. It was. On a chance that the plans were under it, we tried to move the thing, but it wouldn't give more than an inch.

We gave up on the chifferobe and went through the desk. It was empty. Then we crawled under the bed. Nothing. Finally we climbed out to the porch and nearly fell through the rotted floor, so we climbed back in and decided not to check any more bedroom porches. It's a long drop to the ground, and we did not intend to wind up like Mrs. Jennings's father.

We were just climbing inside when Miss Sally found us. I knew she'd be furious that we'd been on the porch. My mother would have a fit.

But she didn't notice the fact we'd just near killed ourselves. It was the filth on us that got her.

And we sure were dirty. We looked like something that came out of a coal mine. I tell you, that attic of Angel's was a dust box. Somebody ought to clean it one of these days.

"Don't touch another thing," Miss Sally shrilled. "Downstairs. Downstairs to wash."

"Do as she says," Angel grumbled. "She's a clean freak."

All the way to the kitchen Miss Sally yelled. What disgraces we were. Filthy. Filthy. And touching that beautiful furniture. Shame. On and on until, by the time we arrived at the kitchen, she was all yelled out. She grabbed a bar of brown soap from under the sink and gave it to Angel.

"Wash," she commanded.

Angel returned the soap.

"We're only going to get dirtier," she explained. "We're going to the cellar."

"What on earth for?" Miss Sally asked. "You've been there a thousand times."

"We're exploring. Billy's never seen the cellar."

Miss Sally wasn't happy, but as long as we weren't going to dirty the house, she let us go.

Angel took a flashlight from the hook. We'd need it, for the only light that worked in the cellar was in the furnace room.

Down we went. Down, down to a dungeon of brick walls and stone floors. The spiderwebs were swept away, but dirt clung like paint to the walls and windows. Sick splatters of light tried to penetrate the windows, but failed miserably. If it weren't for Angel's flashlight we might as well have been blind.

"Who'd store plans in a place like this?" I asked. "Let's go back upstairs."

"I'm sick of looking for those plans," Angel replied. "Besides, if we go upstairs Miss Sally'll make us clean up, and that'll waste half the day. Let's try to find the room without them."

"What makes you think it's down here?"

"It's got to be. If the Civil-War Seeley handled as many guns as those orders said he did, he wouldn't have kept them upstairs. He'd have hidden them down here, and snuck them out somehow."

"But Jeremiah said he did his business in a guest house. He'd have kept the guns there. Don't you think?"

"Don't say that," Angel replied. "If he did, we're sunk. The room's got to be down here. I say there's a trap door on the floor somewhere."

She ran her light in straight patterns up and down the floor. The cellar was so big, I figured we'd take the rest of the day to cover it.

"We ought to be more scientific," I suggested, following her. "If we're not going to look for the plans, let's go back to your office and get the map. Maybe there's a clue on the map."

"The map!" Angel exclaimed, stopping in her tracks. "I'd forgot all about it! With all the stuff going on today, I forgot about it. I don't know how. I've been studying it so much it's part of my brain."

She found a broom in the corner near the steps, and with the handle, drew the map in the dust on the wall.

"Let's see," she said, standing back. "The money's not in the path." She crossed it out. "And it's not at the dead tree." She did the same. "The only thing left are these vertical lines in front. What do you think they mean?"

"Beats me," I said. "Maybe Waterman's pen wasn't working and he scratched a few lines to get it to go."

"Don't be ridiculous," Angel returned. "Everything on a treasure map means something. It's like a rebus, and you have to figure it out. Now. The lines go below the path."

"And they're in front of it," I added.

"Below the path and in front of it."

"Which means the room is below the path and in front of it, right at the corner of this house," I said.

"Can't be," Angel said. "We'd have found it with the densitometer yesterday."

"Then it's under the cellar at the corner. Look how far down the lines go."

It was true. The lines went clear off the bottom of the paper, a good four inches below the end of the path. Considering the path was actually over two hundred feet long, that scaled the room mighty deep.

"You're right. The room *is* under this house," Angel said at last. "No wonder we didn't figure that. Waterman tricked us. He put the path and the moon and the tree on the map to mix us up. He didn't want us to find the treasure before he had a chance to get back to it. Come on."

Angel led the way past the furnace room to the very back of the cellar. Against the wall, in the far corner, stood a chifferobe.

"It's under that," she said, trying to sound calm.

"Then let's go."

We tried to push the chifferobe away, but it wouldn't budge.

"I'll bet it's bolted," I said.

"Then there's a trap door in it," Angel replied.

We opened the chifferobe, but found no door, just an ordinary wood floor.

But there was something that made this chifferobe different from the others in Angel's house. This one had no drawers, and no crossbar for hanging clothes. The only carpentry inside was a thick vertical panel which divided the chifferobe evenly into two parts. It was almost like two separate closets.

"Got to be a way to get through this floor," Angel said.

"There is. We'll bash it in."

While she held the light, I searched for something to break through the floor. I found a heavy pipe.

"This'll do."

Again and again I hammered the floor with the end of the pipe. The cellar echoed with each thud. I hammered so hard my hands vibrated, making the veins in my arms tingle.

Finally the floor split, but it was a long time before it splintered enough for the pipe to break through. The wood in this old piece of furniture was thick.

I gave one last heave, expecting the pipe to fall from my hands as it cut to the secret room, but it didn't. Instead it smacked into stone, burning my hands with the vibration of the impact.

"Wrong place," I said, rubbing my hands.

I pulled up the pipe and started again on the other side of the vertical panel, but hammering there wasn't so hard, for the floor was already weak. After only a few pounds, it separated from the chifferobe and fell to the stone floor.

Yes. The chifferobe floor fell to the cellar floor. There wasn't any room under it. To be sure I banged again and heard the thud that resounds when something solid is hit.

"Where's the secret room?" I snarled.

"I don't know. It should be there."

Angrily I tossed the pipe behind me. It clattered and rolled to a stop.

"I knew I shouldn't have stayed in this treasure business," I said. "All we do is come to dead ends."

"That's always the way," Angel sighed. "In Mexico my father had to go through five miles of tunnels before he found a cache of Aztec gold. And you know where he found it? In a lake. The last tunnel led to a lake and they had to get professional divers to dive for it."

"So what's Mexico got to do with your cellar?" I asked.

"Just that the treasure is here. Maybe it's behind the chifferobe."

"It can't be. The densitometer would have found it. Remember?"

"Not if it's just a tiny room, and low. It could be under the bushes. We never went under the bushes yesterday."

That was true. At the corner of Angel's house are thick yews. It had been impossible to go under them with the densitometer.

We could have saved ourselves a lot of time by tapping the back of the chifferobe for a hollow sound, but never thought of it. We did think to look for a secret button, a hidden latch, something which would open the back. I didn't want to pound any more walls unless it was necessary.

"Besides," I reasoned, "if this room were

used all the time, there had to be a way to get in and out of it without wrecking the chifferobe."

I climbed in on the right and pressed the corners, then slid my hand across the back. When nothing moved I checked the dividing board.

Then I noticed that the back of the chifferobe wasn't all one piece. One board fit behind the other, neatly concealed by the vertical panel. It was such a perfect fit that no one would find it without looking carefully.

"It's a sliding door!" Angel exclaimed.

Sure seemed that way, but how were we to get it open? I'd already pushed everything that could be pushed.

"You didn't check the panel," Angel said. "Here, hold the light."

I got out and Angel got in. Slowly she moved both hands from top to bottom of one side, then she went out of the chifferobe and into the other side. It was near the floor of the other side that she hit what looked like a knot in the wood.

"Look. It goes in," she said.

The wall behind her began to move. Slowly at first, then, with a quick spring, one side of the back slid behind the other. The door had opened!

We'd found it, an opening in the cellar wall, five feet by three feet, one half the width of the chifferobe. It had been there all the time — all the time we dug the path, all the time Waterman lived in the house, all the time Mrs. Jennings's family lived there, and no one knew.

"Waterman knew," Angel said. "He's the one who made the noises and turned on the lights."

"This is where he hid from the police," I gulped.

"Don't worry. He's not here now," Angel said, shining her light inside. "Remember what Mr. Robertson said. He's long since gone."

I wanted to believe her, but something inside me churned. If it weren't for what we saw, I would have run.

Not that what we found was so fantastic. It was merely a narrow landing to a stairway. It was made of brick, wide enough for a man to stand, but small enough to feel cramped. Angel and I both crowded in it and peered down the stairs. They were so deep we couldn't see where they ended.

I wondered how many people had walked down those steps. Had Waterman? Was he still there? Was his money? Had he booby-trapped the steps? Would we slip on rubber balls if we went down?

11

BURIED ALIVE

We didn't get down those steps right away. Miss Sally and my mother ruined it.

My mother phoned and asked Miss Sally to remind me I had a ball game that night. When Miss Sally opened the cellar door to call, Angel and I were on the landing behind the chifferobe. We were petrified she'd come down and find our secret.

Miss Sally told me later that she'd never have come into that cellar. She'd gone in once and couldn't abide the dirt. But Angel and I were so determined to keep everyone away from our treasure that we panicked.

We doused our light and snuck through the chifferobe, closing the doors quietly. Then we felt our way past the furnace room. When we were certain Miss Sally would never guess what part of the cellar we'd been in, we returned her calls.

"About time," she replied. "I was wondering if you two had been murdered down there."

When she got a load of our condition she threw me out, and dragged Angel up the back stairs to shower. Her father was coming home. He should never see her like that.

I couldn't blame Miss Sally. If we looked like coal miners after the attic, I don't know what we looked like after the cellar.

There was no porch outside Angel's bathroom, no way she could sneak out and get back. Miss Sally guarded the door while she showered and changed. Angel told me that she tried every trick in the book, but couldn't get Miss Sally away from guarding that door.

I myself started back, pried open the cellar window and was about to climb through, when my mother appeared.

"What on earth are you doing?" she asked, perplexed. "Get home and wash up. You'll never make it to the game on time."

It killed me to go home. Even though it was Tadpole's first time pitching, and I knew I shouldn't let him down, it killed me.

During my shower I considered playing sick, but that would be worse. My mother would call the doctor 'cause she'd know I was dying. Under normal circumstances I have to have a fever of 125°F and two broken legs before I don't play.

At any rate, I put on my uniform, ate my supper, and drove to the game with Tadpole and our parents.

Tadpole's father doesn't usually go to the games 'cause he thinks baseball is stupid, but this was Tadpole's big night, and even Mr. Robertson was excited about it.

I tried to keep up the big act, but my heart wasn't in it.

The game was a fiasco. Tadpole pitched fine, but I couldn't keep my mind on the ball. I gave the wrong signals and didn't follow through. I missed pitches. I bobbled. I dropped easy foul tips. By the third inning we were losing five to zip, all because of me.

Tadpole came in and asked if I was all right. I said I was fine, to please just give me a chance.

"I thought you were supposed to give *me* a chance?" he asked. "It's my first game. Remember?"

Poor Tadpole. How was he to know that the only thing on my mind was the money?

Would Angel wait for me to go down those steps? Gosh, I hoped so.

The coach wanted to bench me, but that would be a disgrace. I've been catching Little League since I was ten years old. I asked for another chance.

I can't remember the next three innings. I guess I played better, because we won.

Everyone ran in and slapped Tadpole on the back and told him he was the greatest. He said I was the one who should get the praise, 'cause I'd coached him (exactly as I'd figured), so they all slapped me on the back and said I was the greatest.

Even the coach said, "Billy, I have to hand it to you. If you don't have a career in baseball, you've got one in coaching."

It was my night all right, but I couldn't enjoy it. All I wanted was to get back to Angel's. The team was going for sodas, but I said I didn't feel well.

"Well, go home and get better for Saturday's game," the coach said. "You and Tadpole are a team."

My mother and father came in from the stands. My mother was laughing so hard my father had to help her keep her balance.

"Billy," she said between bursts, "that chocolate dessert you and Angel brought to Mrs. Jennings. . . . Why didn't you tell me it had ants in it? Can you beat that? Mrs. Jennings served chocolate ants to the bridge club!"

Lord. I'd forgotten all about it.

"Everyone raved," Mom continued. "How pretty those platters looked, and how delicious! They told Mrs. Jennings she was the best cook ever, and she said she made the chocolate from a secret recipe. Some secret. Old Jeremiah gave it on his CB report tonight. The whole town's laughing and Harriet Jennings is carrying on like a banshee. Ha ha ha ha ha ha ha."

Even my father laughed. He wiped his eyes and gave his handkerchief to my mother to wipe hers.

"I don't know when I've laughed so hard," my mother said. "You kids better make yourselves scarce around Harriet from now on."

When the team heard about the chocolate ants, I was officially declared super hero of the night. Course, some kids weren't pleased, 'cause their mothers ate the ants, but most fought to get near me.

"To think Angel Wilson is your girl friend," Mike Callahan said, whopping me on the back. "What a lucky guy."

(Mike's mother doesn't play bridge.)

No sense denying Angel was my girl friend, but I sure wished I could get home and find out what she was up to.

Tadpole elected to go to The Station, but I kept saying I had a headache. We dropped the Robertsons off and I went up to bed.

I turned on my light and found Angel plopped on my bed, legs crossed, arms folded behind her head.

"Where'd you play — Japan?" she asked indignantly. "I've been waiting all night."

"You should have come to the game," I replied, throwing my hat on the dresser. "Word's out on your chocolate ants. You're a star."

"Not me — Miss Sally," Angel said, "but I'll take the credit. Come on. Let's go. We don't have time to celebrate yet."

I followed her down the roof and in no time we were back in her cellar. We'd climbed through the very window Tadpole and I had used on Halloween.

Angel'd found miners' helmets with lights on the front that she said her father used in his treasure hunts. She showed me how to turn mine on. The helmet would free us to use both our hands.

We put them on and stepped through the chifferobe. We learned that the sliding door in the back worked on a spring. We were careful to close the doors behind us. We pushed it shut and set the spring again.

"Did you find anything while I was at the game?" I asked, peering down the steps.

"I didn't go down. I couldn't. We're partners. Remember? Anyway, a treasure hunter doesn't explore alone. It's dangerous."

"Well, let's go."

The steps were steep, twenty-six in all. At the bottom was another small landing, the entrance to a tunnel.

"So it wasn't a room after all," Angel exclaimed.

Her voice rang through the tunnel and crashed back.

"It must be long, for an echo like that," she whispered.

"Seeley's tunnel, I bet," I replied. "And if your map is correct, it goes under the path to the dead tree. This is how he got to his guest house."

"Then it's awfully deep, or the densitometer would have picked it up."

The tunnel was high, carved neatly in an arch, and wide enough for us to walk side by side. It was floored with the same stone as the cellar. As I walked my baseball spikes clanked on it, echoing eerily. I wished I'd thought to change them.

We found fresh clumps of dirt on the floor, fallen from the ceiling. I guess the bulldozer had loosened the dirt when it filled the trench this morning.

"Hope the whole thing doesn't cave in on us," Angel whispered.

It was chilly. Angel didn't mind 'cause she was wearing a sweatshirt, but in my baseball uniform I shivered.

The path was straight, but we walked slowly, for I was leery of booby traps.

We were far into the tunnel when we came to an old, rusty wheelbarrow. Even the rubber handles on it were rotted.

"What's a wheelbarrow doing down here?" Angel whispered.

"What had his money in a wheelbarrow?" I returned.

"Old Man Waterman! Mygosh. We've found the money!"

Not so fast. Nothing in the wheelbarrow. Nothing around it, but just behind stood a beam supporting a cross brace at the ceiling.

After we passed it, the tunnel became narrow and low. The walls were no longer smooth, but hewn roughly, with boulders jutting here and there. At least it was quieter to walk on, for the floor was now dirt.

"This wasn't built with the original tunnel," I observed. "It had to be added later."

"A darn sight later," Angel whispered. "I'll bet Waterman did this."

"But why?" I asked. "He had enough tunnel to hide his money. Why would he add on?"

"I don't know, but he did it," Angel replied. "Remember Bugsy's grandmother always complained about his dirty sink?"

Brilliant. What better way to get rid of dirt he didn't want anyone to see, but to wash it down a sink?

I took the lead. We were in Waterman territory and I couldn't trust Angel to know how dangerous that was.

I had to duck under some of the boulders, they were so low. At a few points our heads nearly touched the ceiling. If Old Man Waterman was tall, he'd have bent to come through here. I guess that's where he got his stoop.

We passed a second beam and behind it lay a spade on the floor. I examined it for wires, but didn't find any.

A little ways behind the spade we came to a room. It was totally round, with the ceiling criss-crossed by roots of a tree.

The room was big, easily twenty feet in diameter, I'd say, hacked out of roots. Must have been really hard to do.

It was a grand hiding place, and safe, for the roots of the tree were thick enough to hold the ceiling in place without support. As I studied it, I realized why Old Man Waterman had lengthened Seeley's tunnel. He'd wanted to go under the tree in the field. He'd wanted a safe hideaway for himself down here.

We entered and stood in the middle. Directly in front of us were shelves holding canned food and containers of water. Next to them were boxes of candles and battery lights. I walked over and tried one. It still worked. I kept it on because the shafts of light from our miners' helmets were too narrow to really give us a good view.

Next to the battery lights were a table and chair. On the table was a kerosene lamp, partly filled.

"He probably hid here while the police searched his house," I said. "Then he went back and guarded the place so no one else would bother him."

"Especially you, on Halloween," Angel giggled.

It wasn't funny.

I asked, "If Waterman was here then, where is he now?"

"Not in this room. That's for sure," Angel said.

Obviously she was right, for the room hadn't been used in years. Layers of fine silt covered everything.

I felt something underfoot and bent to see what it was.

"Look!" I cried. "Money!"

I picked it up. It was a packet, marked and wrapped in a bank holder. Fifty hundred dollar bills. Five thousand dollars. We were rich!

I waved the packet at Angel, but she didn't see me 'cause she was counting one of her own.

"How much?" I asked over her shoulder.

"Five thousand. Same as you," she smirked. "I told you we'd find it."

"That's just *part* of it. Where's the rest?"

"Who cares? We'll find it. We found this much."

No doubt about that. We were millionaires.

"Half millionaires," Angel corrected.

You can't imagine what it's like to know, all of a sudden, that you're half a millionaire. It's the most light-hearted feeling in the world. It's the kind of feeling that tells you you don't have to worry about school grades, or college, or a career, 'cause you've got enough money to see you a lifetime. It's the kind of feeling that tells you you can go skiing and camping anytime you want, and get a fifty-dollar catcher's mitt, and buy those new track shoes your mother said were too expensive for a kid your age. It's the kind of feeling that says you can buy your father that boat he wants, and your mother a new car so she doesn't have to buzz around in a blue beetle that's ten years old.

Sure. We'd find the money. We swung our lights until we spotted a path of the stuff.

'One . . . two . . . three. . . . Angel sang, tossing the packets to me as she picked them up. "What's this? Omygosh! Oh, no!"

We'd followed the packets to a pile of ashes near the wall opposite the table. Around it were torn money wrappers.

"You don't think he burned it. Do you?" Angel asked, her voice rising.

"Na," I replied, falling to my knees next to her. "He loved money too much to burn it. He was a miser."

Certainly Waterman hadn't burnt the money. No one in his right mind would burn a million dollars, I thought. Sure gave me a scare to see those ashes, though.

To be certain, we raked the ashes, and with each turn of our fingers our hearts sank. Here a charred piece of bill. There the corner of one that read "100."

We sifted and resifted each square inch. Nothing. Not one whole bill left. Not even half of one. He'd burnt it. He'd burnt all his money.

In disbelief, I stared at Angel, and she returned the look, her dark eyes wide as moons.

"What kind of a nut would burn a million dollars?" I cried, grabbing a handful of ashes, throwing it into the air.

If floated down like dry rain.

"Maybe he didn't burn it all," Angel said hopefully. "Let's look some more."

Again we circled the room, searching first the floor, then the shelves and furniture. Near the table and chair was a cot, covered with an army blanket. As I touched it, Angel shrieked.

A skull rolled to the floor. Its empty eye sockets stared up at me.

I ran from the room so fast that when my head grazed a low boulder in the tunnel and my helmet flew off, I merely ducked, so I wouldn't hit more, and kept on like a quarterback with a firecracker in the seat of his pants. I didn't care that my light was gone and that I couldn't see where I was going. I didn't care when I hit the spade in the tunnel. I ran until I crashed into the beam and fell on my face.

Only then did I think, and then, just enough to know that the tunnel was collapsing on me.

Dirt and rocks and more dirt and more rocks pelted me with such ferocity that if I hadn't instinctively moved my arms to protect my head I would have had my brains bashed in. After a while the pain of the pelting stopped, for I was smothered, and could feel only the heavy weight of a ton of dirt on my back.

I was buried alive. I tried to move my arms, but they were pinned to my head. I tried to move my back, but it was no use. Even my legs were bound under immovable weight. The best I could do was wiggle my toes.

Wiggle I did, and push my feet, and thrust and thrash, but the more I tried to get out, the heavier the load on me.

My lungs throbbed for air. My head spun.

Get out, I kept thinking. Get out. You have to get out. Get air.

Breathe. If I could take one breath. . . . I was suffocating. I was going to die!

In my mind I was the skull that had fallen to the floor, my own teeth grinning weirdly at me, as if to say, "and now you."

Not me. No. Not me.

Breathe. One breath. Please. One breath.

I was so dizzy. So dizzy. Spinning . . . spinning . . . spinning. . . . Flashes of light and dark . . . stars in a black night. . . .

Were my legs moving? Was I moving? Was someone pulling at my feet? Was the load lighter on my back?

Push, Billy. Push. I was so tired.

Vaguely I remember pulling my hands to my sides, pushing up, someone holding my shoulders, pulling me up on my knees as I pushed.

The first deep breath came. Then short gasps. Then long, deep sighs. How good. How very, very good. How very, very good to breathe again. How very, very good to be alive.

I was alive! I was on my knees. I was choking.

Someone was pummeling my back. If she didn't stop soon she would break clear through to my chest.

"Hey! Cut it out!" I wailed.

"You okay, Billy?" Angel cried. "You okay?"

Good old Angel. She'd saved me.

"I'm okay," I laughed, "but if you'd just stop socking me I think I'd be better."

"Put your hands in the air. You'll stop choking."

"But I'm not choking anymore."

"Then put them down. Let me see. Are you in one piece?"

The light from her helmet blinded me, but I felt her hands moving along my face.

"You've a cut on your forehead. It'll be a bump pretty soon. I wish we had some ice.

"You don't feel anything broken? Do you?"

No. I felt in one piece. A bit shaky. My shoulder hurt. I guess that's where I hit the beam.

She helped me to my feet. I swayed with dizziness, but she held me until it went away.

"I was so scared," she sighed. "So scared. I couldn't get the beam off your legs, and when I did, more dirt fell down. I had to dig with my hands. I never dug so hard in my life. It took so long I thought you'd be dead."

So that's what pinned my legs — the beam, but which one? Angel's helmet light didn't show any more than a path behind us and a wall of dirt in front of us.

We started down the path. When Angel tripped on the spade in the dirt we knew we were near Waterman's room, but we also knew we'd have one terrible job digging through the rest of Waterman's tunnel.

"Grab that spade," I said. "We're going to need it."

Angel didn't reply. A sickening rumble overhead sent her racing. I followed at her heels.

12

TRAPPED

I've never been in an earthquake, but I know what it's like, because Angel and I watched one from Waterman's room under the tree. Dirt pounded at the entrance, pouring through, hurling rocks as it went. The room vibrated with its fury, showering layers of dust on us. Then, as quickly as it came, the earthquake stopped.

We waited for the dust to settle. When it did, our spirits sank. We were sealed in.

For a long time neither of us moved, just stood a little numb and a lot scared. How would we get out?

"It's not so bad," Angel finally said. "Every treasure hunter has this happen once in a while. We're lucky. We've got the spade to dig out."

Some luck. I hadn't bargained for this.

At least we were safe. Some small chunks of dirt had fallen from our ceiling, but the roots had held firm. Of course half the room was taken up with dirt from the tunnel.

"We ought to dig straight up," Angel said, "and climb to the field. It'll be easier than trying to make it to Seeley's tunnel."

It made good sense to dig up. We had ten ... maybe fifteen feet to go. Waterman's tunnel was twice as long as that.

Most of the tunnel dirt was damp. I figured if we dug carefully in a slant, we could pack the sides and crawl out as we dug.

We pulled over the chair and set a battery light on it, so neither of us had to hold it. Angel said she'd start because I was still shaky from before.

She was terrible. She didn't shovel, she attacked. Every time she put the spade down she started a new avalanche.

"Will you be more careful," I carped.

"I'm trying. It just won't stop coming."

"Take smaller shovelsful," I said. "You don't have to beat it to death."

The look she gave me I can't put in this book, but she did tame down a bit.

Still the dirt rolled in.

"Where's it coming from?" Angel asked.

I didn't know, but if I didn't take over the shoveling the whole rotten tunnel would be in on us.

"Give me that," I said, grabbing the spade.

"Go ahead, smart aleck. See if you can do any better," she snapped.

Of course I could do better. Anybody could do better.

But I didn't do better. With each shovelful, twice as much dirt fell in. It got so bad I didn't have anyplace to throw the dirt. Already the room seemed much smaller than it had before.

"Told you so," Angel said.

Well, I had it coming to me. No sense fighting about it. The big problem now was to stay alive and get out.

The food was safe. It was on the other side. The cot and table hadn't been touched either.

What worried me was our air supply. Now that the tunnel was sealed, where would we get it?

I poked around the shelf till I found a box of wooden matches. I lit one. It burned evenly. Plenty of air now. How long would it last?

We sat on the floor and tried to figure a way out, but neither of us came up with any ideas, other than if we didn't get one soon, we'd suffocate.

It would be pretty rotten to have to die down here. We wouldn't even have a proper funeral 'cause no one would find our bodies.

The way I see it, if a kid's going to die, he ought to have everybody crying about it, with the priest preaching what a fine boy he was, and the choir breaking up in the middle of the Dies Irae, and anybody who ever did anything mean to him saying he's sorry.

And if *two* kids are going to die, that should be a town affair, with the mayor and the councilpersons at the funeral, and the flags in the school at half mast, and the Little League games canceled, and the Boys Scouts and the Girl Scouts marching behind the caskets, and all traffic stopped, while everybody kneels in solemn prayer.

"Don't worry. Someone will find us before that happens," Angel said.

"Fat chance. Who's going to look under a dead tree?"

Nobody knew we were here. Nobody even knew about the map. We'd been so careful to keep it a secret.

"Miss Sally will tell my father we were in the cellar. He'll go down and find the chifferobe."

"We closed the doors. Remember? Even if he opens them, we closed the back."

"He'll see the floor is broken and figure it out."

"Sure. Now, he's a miracle mind."

There was no doubt about it. We were trapped. How long we would last was anybody's guess.

At the foot of the hill lay the skull that had started the trouble, its bare teeth grinning. I didn't want to see it. I didn't want to think that Angel and I would wind up like that.

Angrily, I picked the skull up and threw it on the cot. When it hit I noticed the blanket wasn't a blanket at all. It was an army coat. The bones of a spine and hands stuck out of it. I looked down and saw shoes — dusty, old, dirt-encrusted shoes, with trousers running to them, molded to the configuration of leg bones.

We'd found Waterman. As everyone promised, he was with his money, but what good did it do him?

"I should have known," Angel said grimly.

I'd never liked Waterman. He was a sour

old man. He was mean and nasty. And why he'd boarded himself in his house I couldn't figure. But this . . . to come to this . . . to let himself die while he burnt his money . . . it was the dregs.

The skull sat grinning on Waterman's chest. I couldn't stand it. I shoved it under the cot.

In the bones of Waterman's hand was another packet of money. When I pulled it away, the bones fell like twigs.

Angel took a blanket from the shelf and covered the skeleton.

To keep ourselves busy, we picked up the money we'd dropped when we ran. Some of it was buried under the avalanche, but we found three packets. Waterman'd nearly succeeded in his job.

"I wonder what killed him," I said, but didn't need a reply, for in the back of my mind I knew. *He'd suffocated.*

"It's all my fault," Angel said. "If I hadn't screamed, you wouldn't have panicked, and we wouldn't be in this mess."

"No," I replied. "I'm the one who knocked down the tunnel. Not you. I lost my head."

Even with Angel's helmet and that one battery light, it was pretty dim. We might figure a way out if we could see better. I got another battery light, turned it on, and hung it on a root. As I did, I remembered something I'd learned in science — that some animals burrow deep under trees. Perhaps there were animal holes letting air in. I looked for them in the ceiling, but didn't find any.

The roots of the ceiling gave me an idea. Why not try to dig through them? The ceiling hadn't collapsed as the tunnel had because the roots had held the dirt in place. They'd probably hold if we dug now.

Angel was all for it.

"We won't have to dig as far, either, because we're starting higher," she said.

Yes. From trying to dig the tunnel, we'd created a good six-foot hill of dirt. We wouldn't have far to go.

I banged around the ceiling until I found a spot where the dirt broke easily. It was near the cot. To reach better I stood on the chair. After the first few chops with the spade, I found that the dirt wasn't soft at all. It was hard as nails.

Angel found a spoon in the food supply. She stood on the table and worked with that. We took turns with the shovel and spoon, but the spoon turned out to be a dud. It kept bending back.

186

Maybe my spikes would do — good steel spikes for which I'd paid thirty dollars from my chore money. I bet they'd be good for breaking the dirt. I took one off and smashed it into the ceiling. It sure beat the spoon.

We banged and smashed until our arms were numb. We stopped to rest and started again.

The opening grew. Our breathing was still easy. If the air held out we had a chance.

We came to a thick root, and hacked the dirt around it. "If this is strong enough we'll use it to climb on," I said. "We'll need a ladder to get up."

It seemed strong. I tested it. Then Angel did. Then both of us together. It was strong, all right.

As the hole grew higher, we began to get in each other's way. We tried rotating in rhythm, one smash with the spade, one with the spike, but that didn't work. One of us was always elbowing the other. So we decided to work one at a time. Since I had the shovel, I started.

The hardest thing in the world is to dig up. You don't have any leverage. All you have is the strength in your arms, and after a while you lose that.

The pain in my shoulders was horrible. My arms ached. My neck throbbed. When I couldn't bear it, I stopped a few minutes to rest, but when I started again the pain came quicker.

I gave the spade to Angel. When she couldn't bear the pain she gave it back.

We were taking shorter shifts. Each time Angel stopped she moaned and rubbed her arms. Each time I started I wondered how I'd raise the shovel over my head. On my last turn I thought my arms would fall off.

I climbed down and handed the spade to Angel.

"I can't," she said wearily.

Her eyes were glassy, her hair straggled. Dirt smeared her face.

Poor Angel. She'd worked as hard as I, and she couldn't be as strong. What did she do that would make her strong enough to hold a spade over her head and bang into a ceiling for what seemed like hours at a time?

She didn't play ball, and she hadn't been swimming all summer. If my arms hurt, hers must have been twice as bad.

"That's okay," I said. "Rest."

But we had to go on, for we couldn't waste

precious air. I got on the table and tried again, but my arms wouldn't work.

Maybe I could use the spade as a lever. I'd put it over the root and pull.

I tried and it worked, but it was discouraging because often the spade hit roots and sent down mere sprinkles of dirt. But it widened the hole enough for me to fit in and sit on the root. Now I could dig without raising my arms so high.

I kept going until I'd cleared all but one thick root. It would be the next rung on our ladder. All I had to do was clear it. The thought gave me new strength, and I began hammering like a machine, but, like a machine, I ran out of gas.

I was so tired I wanted to stay right there, lean back, and sleep. But I couldn't do that. We had to keep on.

Just to climb down hurt. But I made it, and handed the spade to Angel.

"I can't," she said.

She was huddled in a blanket, shivering so that her teeth chattered.

"Maybe if I had something to eat I'd feel better."

She nodded toward the shelves of canned food.

At least Waterman had done one decent thing in his life. He'd loaded the shelves with all kinds of foods. Besides the normal stuff there were tins of crackers, and containers of water.

I found a can opener and opened some beets, then peaches. We finished a tin of crackers and jam. We drank the juice from the beets and peaches, then took water.

Angel felt a lot better. She said she could take her turn at the shovel. I sat in her spot and listened to her work, but after a time I became so cold I had to wrap myself in a blanket.

It occurred to me that if the air was running out I shouldn't be cold. I should be very hot and sweaty. I'd be sleepy, too, but I wasn't.

Why hadn't we used up the air? Where was it coming from?

I was pondering the question when Angel climbed down.

"I'm beat," she said. "Let's rest. If we haven't suffocated by now, we never will."

"You don't mean sleep, do you?" I asked.

"Yes. Sleep. We've got to get some sleep. If I don't get some sleep I'm going to fall on my face."

"But if we do sleep, we might never wake up."

"I know. I've been thinking of that. We might use up our air and wind up like that creepy skeleton over there. But I don't think so, Billy. Really. With all the huffing and puffing we've been doing, the air should have been gone long ago. Anyway, we won't use much sleeping."

It wasn't a matter of discussion, because Angel had already made up her mind. She grabbed another blanket and crawled under the table, which was the only place one could lie flat, unless we wanted to use the cot, and neither of us thought much of sleeping with a skeleton.

I turned out the lights. Gosh. It was dark. Not a shadow. I waited for my eyes to get accustomed to it, but they never did. There were no shadows to see.

The only sound in the room was Angel's steady breathing. I fell asleep listening to it.

I woke. The ground was hard. Angel was breathing next to me. I remembered where I was.

As I groped for the lights, I noticed spots on the wall. I hadn't seen them last night. All had been black. What were they?

I put my hand over one and the spot bounced to my fingers. It was a shadow. A shadow. And a shadow meant light.

I looked to the ceiling and found more. Not strong, no rays, just bits of brown surrounded by black.

But if there was light, there was air! Air! We were getting it from someplace, it didn't matter where. We were getting air!

I felt so good I wanted to dance, and shout, and cry, and scream. I wanted to hug Angel and shake her and tell her, "Angel, we're okay. We've got air. We've got all the air in the world. We don't have to worry. We can dig for a month of Sundays. We're okay, Angel. We're okay."

I shook her.

"Angel. Wake up! Wake up. We've got air!"

I shook her again, and pulled her up, and in the process banged her head on the table, but that was okay because she'd heard me, and so she didn't bother to yell, "Ouch."

"Look, Angel. Look! See? Shadows on the wall!"

"I'm looking," she cried. "Omygosh! Aren't they the most beautiful things you ever saw in your life?"

192

Beautiful? That wasn't the word! Gorgeous. Marvelous. Fantastic.

Lord. It was good to poke at them, watching them bounce from our fingers to the wall.

It killed us to eventually turn on the lights, but we were so hungry we had to. Those shadows gave us whopping big appetites.

Breakfast was canned pears, asparagus, chicken soup (yucky when it's cold), and crackers, with lots of water.

"Not as good as Miss Sally's crumpets," I chuckled.

"I prefer cinnamon ants myself," Angel returned.

We went back to work. I hung a battery light in the hole, so I could see where I was going.

The hole was beginning to look like an upright tunnel at least four feet high with two fine roots to sit on. The second was bigger than the first, and crisscrossed by smaller ones I had a tough time breaking. I finally did, and hacked steadily until I came to a third root. This one was huge.

My arms were throbbing again, but I wouldn't pay attention. I'd seen a show on TV in which people walked on hot coals without getting burned because they didn't think about it. If they could do that, I could push a spade.

Terrific. It was working. If only I could get around this root.

The pain came again, worse. I couldn't keep my mind off it. So much for walking on burning coals. Better let Angel take over.

I climbed down and threw a blanket over my shoulders. I rubbed my arms, and wiggled my fingers until the numbness wore away. Ah. That was better. As long as I didn't try to raise them, I'd be okay.

Let's see. What else to eat? This looked good. Plum pudding. Thank you, Mr. Waterman. Thank you very much. I hadn't had plum pudding since Christmas.

"I can't get through this root," Angel hollered.

"Go around it," I munched.

"I can't."

"Go sideways then."

"I can't. I tried. On one side there's enough roots to choke you, and on the other there's this big one. I think it's the tree trunk."

"Keep working. You'll find something."

The plum pudding was the same brand as my mother's, but not as good cold. I'd have to tell her that. She'd be pleased to know that she could do something right in the kitchen, even if it was heating a can of pudding.

Angel's shovel clanked steadily on the wood. She'd been up there longer than I. No shirk, that Angel.

The clanking stopped, and she slid down.

"There's no dirt left. It's all wood. No matter where I try I can't get through," she said, rubbing her arms.

I don't know why I got mad at her, but I did.

"You're crazy," I said. "Give me the shovel. I'll do it myself."

But Angel wasn't crazy. There was no dirt left, just little pockets here and there, but none wide enough for us to slide through.

I tried to bash in some of the roots, but even the smallest ones were bigger than a man's leg, and hard. They wouldn't chip no matter how hard I hit them.

I checked that big one. Of all the luck. It was the trunk, all right. The tap root. Well, it wasn't going to get me.

I banged, and banged, and banged. The harder I banged the madder I got. I was so mad I cried, but I kept on banging.

Finally I gave up. It was no use. All I'd accomplished was giving myself a whopping headache.

If only we had a saw. Maybe we could use the tops of those food cans we'd opened. Ridiculous. How can you cut through wood the size of a man's leg with the cover to a can of plum pudding?

But we had no choice. It was the only way.

Wait. I'd heard something. What was it?

Tapping. Tapping. Coming down the trunk I'd heard tapping. A steady tap, tap, tap. When I put my hand on the root I felt the vibration.

Someone was up there. Someone had heard me!

I banged three times with the spade.

Three taps back.

I banged one short. Three long.

Back it came.

"Angel, someone's up there," I shouted. "Somebody knows we're here!"

"Get down. I don't believe you."

I got down and Angel got up, but I stayed on the table to listen.

She banged dum dum dumdum dum. Dum Dum.

It thumped back.

"He's signaling," she laughed. "I told you they'd find us."

She banged again, but this time no reply came forth.

She tried again No reply.

She banged. She screamed. She banged. She got down and I got up.

I banged . . . and screamed . . . and banged. Nothing.

He'd gone away. He had heard us, but he'd gone away. How could he? How could he go away and leave us down here? How could anyone be so cruel?

Suddenly I was tired. I was so tired that if I wasn't in that hole under the tree with roots to hold me, I'd have fallen down. I leaned against the tap root and cried.

13

TAPPING AGAIN

I don't know when the tapping started again. I had climbed down from the hole and was shivering under the table with Angel. We had checked our food and found it enough for eternity. We had decided to start another tunnel as far from the tap root as we could get. This time we'd work sideways, for the roots would be thinner if we worked out from the trunk.

But first we had to rest, for we were exhausted. Worse than the exhaustion was the cold. It hadn't bothered us much before, but suddenly it was terrible. I didn't know why. I figured that we had to be awfully deep to be this cold.

How far we were from the surface neither of us would venture, but as I wrapped my arms around myself and felt the ache in every muscle I wondered how we could ever dig again.

When the taps once again sounded from the root we thought we were dreaming. We listened for more than a minute before Angel jumped up.

"It's real," she said. "He's back."

She climbed up the hole and answered. I stood under her on the table, my heart pounding.

Angel returned the steady one, one-two-one, one-two pattern so many times I found myself becoming furious with whoever was up there. Didn't he know the predicament we were in? Didn't he know we were trapped? Why was he playing games with us?

Suddenly the room rocked. It was as if a meteor had hit it. Angel jumped from the ceiling.

"He's trying to kill us," she cried.

We dove under the table and huddled together while explosion after explosion rocked the room. The shelf holding the food fell over. The table shook. The chair fell on its side. The battery light tumbled from the hole, bouncing from the table to the ground and going dead. Angel's helmet slipped over her

face, shining on the floor, which was a whirl-
wind of dirt. She didn't bother to set it
straight. I suppose she was just as pleased
not to see what was going on.

The explosions stopped. Angel righted her
helmet and we waited for what was to come,
and what was to come came quickly, a hissing
sound from the ceiling.

"Oh, no! A bomb," I groaned barely audi-
bly, for my throat was stuck.

We buried our heads in each other's shoulders, waiting for the bomb to explode. When
nothing hapened, Angel peered out and tilted
her light to the sound.

"It's air!" she exclaimed jubilantly. "When
somebody is trapped underground they send
air. They know we're here, and they're coming to get us."

We jumped on the table and scrambled
with each other for a turn at the beautiful
air. It smelled so good. It tickled. It was
wonderful.

We heard a whirr. As the sound grew
closer, a big chunk of dirt fell from the ceiling. Once again we climbed under the table
for protection, but this time we weren't
frightened.

It wasn't long before a telephone dangled past us to the floor. It wasn't exactly a telephone, but rather a speaker to a CB set.

I grabbed it, and pressed the button.

"Hello?" I shouted. "Hello. Hello. Can you help us?"

Automatically I released the button for a reply.

"Yes. We'll get you up. Don't worry. Who's down there?"

"It's me, Billy Beak, and Angel Wilson. The tunnel caved in."

A new voice came across.

"Billy, this is Mr. Wilson. Are you all right?"

Angel grabbed the mike.

"Oh, Daddy, it's awful," she cried. "It's just awful. The tunnel caved in and the skeleton is on the cot and the money's all burnt and we're so cold and we're so tired and my arms hurt and we can't dig anymore 'cause the roots are too thick. Oh, Daddy. . . ."

Angel was so choked up, I took the mike.

"Mr. Wilson," I said. "We're just fine. We're cold, but not as bad as before. No. We don't need food, something hot maybe . . . no. We're not hurt. Honest. We're not hurt."

I explained what had happened, and gave every detail I could think of about the room.

Mr. Wilson said they'd have to cut a shaft next to the room to get us out. They wouldn't chance cutting through the room because it might cave in on us. It would take a long time, but they would drill a wider opening and send us warm food and drink.

He told us to stay as far from the tunnel as we could. Then he put my father on.

I can be very strong when I talk to somebody else's father, but mine . . . I cried almost as hard as Angel.

Yes. I was all right . . . yes. We'd be patient . . . yes. I'd love hot chocolate.

I think he was crying, too. His voice kept cracking.

My mother got on. I cried again.

I loved her, too . . . I knew we were in a terribly dangerous situation . . . we'd stay away from the cave-in.

"Oh, Billy. My beautiful Billy."

I hoped nobody up there heard her say that. I'd never live it down, but it sure sounded good, like I was a little kid again, and she could solve every problem in my world.

Angel talked to her father again, and then to Miss Sally.

The phone went up, and, as they'd promised, a larger hole was drilled. Then hot chocolate came down, and warm muffins and eggs. And vitamins. Can you beat that? I'm in a hole under a tree and my mother sends me vitamins!

Angel had stopped crying. She laughed about the vitamins and said sarcastically, "Oh, Billy, my beautiful Billy."

I wanted to cream her.

We moved the cot with Waterman's skeleton to the center of the room. Angel kicked the skull in the dirt of the hill, but I picked it up and put it under the blanket. We'd have to go out through that hill, and I didn't want to trip over any man's skull.

We sat where the cot had been, 'cause that was the farthest from the cave-in.

For lunch they sent us pizza. Not bad.

"Isn't this exciting?" Angel chirped, pulling the chewing-gum cheese. "Now you know why I want to be a treasure hunter."

How'd a sensible guy like me get involved with such a crazy girl?

For a long time it seemed as though nothing was happening. I kept calling up, but I guess everybody there was so busy with the rescue that they forgot to man the mike. Then the hill where the entrance had been began to sink. Bit by bit we watched it go down. It was only by watching that hill that we knew they were working, for we couldn't hear the shovels.

Finally we heard scraping behind the hill. A shovel broke through. Then another. Soon there was a hole large enough for a man's head.

"Anybody home?" someone called.

"We're here!" we chorused.

A man crawled into our room. We didn't know him. We'd never before seen his face, but, as Angel said, we'd never forget it. You don't forget the first face you see after you've given yourself up for dead.

"You kids okay?" he asked, his eyes gleaming.

"We're fine. Just get us out of here."

I followed Angel through the opening to a wide, vertical shaft, something like a well. When I looked up, I couldn't believe how deep we were — over twenty feet, easy, with blue sky looming.

The rescuers had rigged a pulley, sort of a vertical breeches buoy. Angel went in first. I can't say that was all right with me, because all I wanted was to get out of that hole, but it wasn't wrong either. I'd never have been able to leave her last.

I heard the cheers when she reached the top, but didn't pay attention. I was too busy watching that buoy come back again for me.

"In you go," the man said, strapping me in.

Slowly they cranked me up. At first I watched the top of the hole, and then the sunlight, but then it became so strong my eyes couldn't bear it. I looked down to the blackness where I'd been. I could barely discern the figure of the man standing there.

I heard the cheers before I saw the crowd — screams, and claps, and whistles. I felt the ground under my feet and stood. Two men unleashed me.

The whole town was there, and then some, a blur before my eyes. I felt my mother putting her arms around me, kissing me, holding me, crying all the time.

"Billy, my beautiful Billy. Thank heaven."

My father hugged me, too. We all hugged each other and cried. I'm not ashamed I cried. They were the happiest tears of my life.

Jeremiah Cleary ran up and near shook off my hand.

"I knew you'd make it, Billy Boy. You and that spunky girl friend of yours. Best story ever."

Tadpole Robertson and Mike Callahan whopped me on the back. Bugsy Schmitt socked me in the arm. Junior Jennings came up and said, "You can thank me, Billy. I saved you."

The creep.

A thousand faces smiled at us. Reporters flashed their cameras. TV men from all thirteen channels whirred. Every time I looked up, a camera was in my face.

What cameras were not fixed on me were on Angel, who wasn't far away. She was so cloaked by Miss Sally and her father that she could barely get an arm past them to wave to me, but she did, and I waved back.

Gosh. She was grimy. I suppose I looked the same myself, but I couldn't see without a mirror. Still, she was beautiful. The most beautiful girl I've ever seen, or ever will.

The press crowded in for an interview, but Mr. Wilson refused. He said it was no time to ask two kids questions they were too tired to answer.

They gave up on us only after the rescue

squad brought up Waterman's skeleton. You should have heard the gasps.

"You mean you were with that thing all the time?" Tadpole asked.

"It's just a bunch of bones," I said nonchalantly.

I was myself again. No more emotion stuff. A little goes a long way.

First Aid tried to get me on the stretcher to take me to the hospital, but my father wouldn't hear of it.

"I'll call my own doctor," he roared. "My son comes home with me."

My mother said my father was acting like a nitwit. They were about to battle the matter when Dr. Scardella came from the crowd and assured everyone he'd check me thoroughly, and would personally escort me to the hospital if I needed it.

Actually, I was fine. Aside from a bump on the head, a sore shoulder, and aching arms, all I needed was a long, hot bath, which I got after the doctor checked every inch of me, from tip of head to toenails.

And then to bed. I was never so happy to have one. My mother had it ready, sheet down and two soft pillows.

I didn't wake up until night. I ate supper watching myself and Angel on the 11 o'clock news.

Imagine being on TV. We were celebrities!

14

POST MORTEM

The next day I learned how we had been saved.

Junior Jennings couldn't get any sleep because his mother had made such a racket about the chocolate ants. His father went to a motel, but Junior was stuck in the house, so he took his sleeping bag outside. He wound up under the dead tree. In the morning, the noise of my banging at the tap root woke him. He got so mad he thumped back with a rock. He was too sleepy to realize what had happened when I returned the signal. He just kept banging back and forth. Then, when it dawned on him that someone under that tree was answering his hammers, he was terrified. He thought it was Waterman's ghost.

He hobbled as fast as he could, but not home. Not with his mother carrying on the way she was. He went to the Wilsons. They owned the tree, and it was their ghost.

Miss Sally could make neither head nor tail of Junior's babbling, so Mr. Wilson came down. To set Junior's mind at rest, he took him back to the tree.

In the backyard, Mr. Wilson found the depression from the tunnel collapse, and got suspicious. In his line of work he'd seen things like this before.

When they reached the tree everything was quiet. Mr. Wilson tapped a code. When Angel finally replied, he knew someone was trapped under there.

Junior was convinced that nobody alive was under that tree, so Mr. Wilson had to do some tall talking to get him to stay and keep tapping while he called for help. Scared as he was, Junior stayed. They still didn't know it was us.

The rest is history, but I must now add that I will never again call Junior Jennings a creep.

But then Junior isn't a creep anymore. His mother left town right after the chocolate ant episode, and his father started spending more time with Junior. He even took him camping the other day.

Mrs. Jennings still writes to Junior from time to time, but she'll never come back. My mother says it's better for her that way. How could she be happy living near so many bad memories?

We never learned why Mrs. Jennings's father sold the estate to Waterman, and then committed suicide. Under the ashes of the money were found the remains of ledgers, but the pages were too burnt and scattered to reconstruct.

My father thinks that Waterman blackmailed Mr. Seeley. He says a lot of dirty business went on during the Depression. My mother says it's a sorry mystery that would be better left unsolved.

The Sunday after our rescue we celebrated with a grand dinner at the Wilsons'.

The first order of business was to settle the treasure money the workmen had recovered. While the grownups chatted in the den, Angel led me into her room and showed me all the bills we had to pay.

Five thousand for the rescue operation,

and to excavate the tree and fill the yard; two thousand for Bugsy's IOU; one thousand reward to Junior for saving our lives.

"That leaves eleven thousand, five hundred each," Angel said. "My father wrote you a check."

It wasn't a million, but it was better than nothing. I knew I'd have to put it in the bank for college. You can't live your life on eleven thousand dollars!

Back in the den, Mr. Wilson was waiting for us, with a bottle of champagne, vintage superyear, which he'd been saving for a special occasion.

"Before I pop this, I have to tell you all that I learned from the coroner," he said. "That skeleton under the tree *was* Old Man Waterman. The dental plates proved it."

"I can't see why they bothered to investigate," my mother remarked. "Who else would it be? What I'd like to know is how he died."

"They have a theory," Mr. Wilson explained. "They believe the room was airtight, like a bomb shelter, right after Waterman dug it. Then, when he burnt his money, he probably lit that kerosene lamp, and poisoned his air."

"You mean he committed suicide?" I asked.

"I doubt that. If he'd wanted to commit suicide, he would have destroyed *all* the money before he did it. I'll venture he didn't know what was happening. He felt sleepy and lay down on the cot to rest."

That made sense to me. Hadn't we found a packet of bills in Waterman's hand?

"If the air in the room was poisoned, how come we didn't die from it?" Angel asked.

"Easy," Mr. Wilson replied. "After the tree died, the roots shrunk and loosened the soil. Then, insects and animals cut through to let in clean air. You kids would never have suffocated down there."

"I guess if nobody had found us we'd have died of old age," I observed. "Or starved."

"Gives me the chills," my mother said.

Mr. Wilson popped the champagne, and poured it around, but my father made the toast.

"To Angel and Billy, who are worth more than any man's million dollars."

"Still and all, it sure would be nice if we had that million," I remarked, sipping the bitter champagne.

"But if we have to choose between you and

that million, we'll take you," my mother laughed.

Amen.

"You know," Angel remarked, "I feel sorry for Waterman. Maybe if he had somebody to care about him, maybe if that lady Jeremiah talked about hadn't jilted him, he wouldn't have died the way he did, burning his money so no one would get it."

"Nonsense," my father retorted. "Waterman was twisted long before that lady left him, and he never did a thing to untwist himself. Each one of us is jilted many times in life, but we keep on caring."

Frankly I wished the conversation would change. I'd had enough of Waterman for a lifetime. I was happy when Miss Sally arrived to usher us to the table.

Since we were only six, we ate in the small dining parlor off the kitchen. Miss Sally outdid herself, and promised my mother some recipes, which struck me as funny because I knew she'd never use them.

"Tell me, is your house really haunted?" I asked Mr. Wilson, spooning sherbet between the appetizer and entree.

"Not that I know of," he replied. "We haven't had any strange occurrences here."

"Told you so," Angel gloated.

"But Tadpole and I heard Waterman's voice on Halloween. And a ball came down the stairs on us."

I told the grown-ups about the incident. After I'd finished, my mother said, "Then maybe Old Man Waterman wasn't *all* bad. Maybe he had to do one decent thing before his soul could rest."

"It's possible," Mr. Wilson said. "As an archaeologist I've seen too much in my travels to disbelieve anything."

"An archaeologist!" I exclaimed. "*She* told me you were a treasure hunter. She said she wanted to be one just like you. That's how we got into this mess."

Angel choked.

"*She* has a vivid imagination at times," Mr. Wilson chuckled.

He turned to Angel.

"How are you going to get out of that one?"

"Well, you *are* a treasure hunter, sort of. Aren't you?" Angel grinned.

Miss Sally served the lamb, and sauce, and

beans, and potatoes, and a hundred other things I can't remember. For a while we were so busy eating we didn't talk. Angel was the first to finish.

As she put down her fork she said to her father, "Now that I'm a treasure hunter, I can go with you on a hunt."

"It isn't a hunt. It's a dig," her father corrected, "and I'm afraid you'd find one quite boring."

"Oh, dear," Angel sighed. "Now I'll have to find another treasure on my own."

Mr. Wilson poured another glass of champagne and drank it down in one gulp.

"In that case I'd better take you with me to Egypt," he said. "There's no telling what you'd get into if I left you here."

"You're not going to dump me in another boarding school, are you?" Angel asked.

"No," her father winked. "You'll be right with me on the expedition, where I can keep an eye on you. Who knows, you might find that lost tomb. According to my hieroglyphics the pharaoh buried there had an enormous treasure."

"Great!" Angel exclaimed. "Can we take Billy?"

It was my turn to choke. I didn't want to find any more tombs — Egyptian, American, or anything else — so I was happy when my father declared I was staying right here where I belonged.

Miss Sally brought two desserts — one a strangely familiar chocolate, cut into figures of diamonds, hearts, spades, and clubs, all fixed on a circular platter with a crab apple in the middle and mint sprigs around. When I saw it I turned green.

"That's not the last platter from Mrs. Jennings's bridge?" I gulped.

"You'll never know unless you taste it," Miss Sally chortled.

"Try one," Angel giggled, helping herself to a handful.